Books by Alina

The Frost Brothers
- Eating Her Christmas Cookies
- Tasting Her Christmas Cookies
- Frosting Her Christmas Cookies

The Svensson Brothers
- After His Peonies
- In Her Candy Jar
- On His Paintbrush
- In Her Pumpkin Patch
- Between Her Biscuits
- After Her Fake Fiancé
- In Her Jam Jar
- After Her Flower Petals

Weddings in the City
- Bridezillas & Billionaires
- Wedding Bells & Wall Street Bros
- Marriage in a Minute
- Flowers & Financiers

Check my website for the latest news:
http://alinajacobs.com/books.html

THE HATE Date

A Romantic Comedy

THE HATE DATE

ALINA JACOBS

Summary: Dating when you're a six-foot-tall girl is not easy. Each of Belle's dates is worse than the last—especially since they keep getting crashed by a six-foot-five handsome billionaire with a huge ego who is determined to make her already crazy life even worse. Or maybe better because he is REALLY good in bed!

This book is a work of fiction. Names, characters, places, and incidents either are products of the author's imagination or are used fictitiously. Any resemblance to actual events or locales or persons, living or dead, is entirely coincidental.

Copyright ©2021 by Adair Lakes, LLC.
All rights reserved, including the right to reproduce this book or portions thereof in any form whatsoever.

*To my many succulents that I can't
seem to keep alive. RIP.*

*I hate Shakespeare and Gosling
and cakes with white frosting*
-Kelsea Ballerini

CHAPTER 1
Belle
♡ ♡ ♡

My mom always told me to tell guys I was five feet twelve and not six feet tall.

"You don't want to scare them off!" she would remind me. "Men don't want tall girls."

But it wasn't like lying about being six feet tall made me *not* six feet tall. I wasn't just taller than most men—I towered over them.

The worst thing about being tall was the comments, and not just from the guys I had dated who would stare at me over drinks, flinching at every motion I made as if they were afraid I was about to sprout up another five inches in front of them.

No, it was also the all-too-common "How's the weather up there?" (Still raining, just like it is five inches below my head). Or the random "You should be a model!" (No, Karen, I shouldn't because I like to eat my weight in fettuccine alfredo). Or the always obnoxious "OMG, how did you get so tall?" (Blame my parents; I sure did.)

My five-foot-nine mom would always sigh when she looked up at me and say, "I don't understand why you're so tall."

Really, *Dr.* Diana Frost? Despite your two PhDs, you have failed to grasp the rudimentary concept that tall person plus tall person makes tall person—tall boys *and tall girls*. My mom had probably thought that her family was going to be like one of those sibling groups in the romance novels I would sneak at night, in which the whole puppy pound of brothers was big and tall, and the one lone sister was short and petite, and her brothers all looked after her and were protective of her.

Ha! I wish!

My brothers were the worst. They were more of a feral cat colony than a basket of puppies—stealing my stuff, fighting, and complaining.

It had been a good thing I was tall. Too busy with their careers to raise six children and too concerned about what the neighbors would say to hire a nanny, my parents left yours truly to single-handedly raise their five very tall, very large, sons. And I hadn't done it because I was sugar and spice and everything nice. I had ruled with an iron fist.

You definitely wanted to be tall and strong when wrestling down a smelly five-foot-eight fourth grader who wouldn't stop playing video games to come eat dinner, or when shot-putting a six-foot-one high school senior's hockey skates at him when he left them in the hallway for the twentieth time.

Sigh. *Praying hands.*

I had been more of a mother to my five younger brothers than our own mother had been. I didn't resent them—after all, I was their big sister. I would always rescue my brothers. That was my thing. Because what else was a six-foot woman to be except for the rescuer?

She definitely wasn't the princess.

I tried to channel that badass rescuer energy as I jogged in the cold along the Hudson River side of Manhattan Island.

I am a warrior. I am a boss.

Except that I hated running. I would much rather be in bed with a book and a bowl of popcorn with Turtle Tracks ice cream at the ready.

As I huffed down the concrete running path, I watched the water. The city had spent the last few years cleaning it up. Now, in warmer weather, people would be swimming, scuba diving, kayaking, and doing other water sports in the river. Not that the sheltered New York urbanites could handle their newfound water sports access. Just last summer, I saved a kid who had been drowning.

In fact…

I peered at the water. Something human-shaped bobbed up and down about a hundred feet out. His head was back, eyes closed, head and shoulders going under the water for a brief moment then back up.

"Hey!" I yelled, cupping my hands around my mouth, "You okay?"

The man wearing the black diving suit didn't respond. I looked around. There wasn't anyone else in the linear park. It was New Year's Day and freezing cold.

The cold didn't bother me. Which was great because clearly that diver needed to be rescued.

I shrugged off my thin long-sleeved shirt, capri running pants, and tennis shoes then dove into the water. Shards of ice pricked my skin as I swam toward the drowning man.

There were times—well, most times—when I hated being the tallest girl, especially since my height hadn't come with model thinness. I was no Princess Diana. I was built like a pioneer woman or a medieval lady knight.

But now I was glad to have my strength. The man was large, and if I were any smaller, I might not be able to drag him to shore.

Once I was a few feet away, I submerged myself in the water to come up under him—the proper technique for rescuing a drowning person—and grabbed him under the armpits.

He started writhing.

Sometimes during a rescue, drowning people panic and try to climb on top of the rescuer. A good pop on the sternum usually stuns them enough to get them to stop.

"Fuck!" the man roared when I used my knuckles to dig into the bone of his breastplate. It was also through a good bit of solid muscle, which I couldn't fixate on because the diver turned on me in the water, furious.

"Are you fucking out of your mind? Where did you come from?" Gray eyes the color of the winter sky glared at me. "Why are you attacking me?"

"I'm rescuing you!" I sputtered, treading water. "You were drowning!"

"No, I'm not!" he declared.

"Your face was half submerged in the water," I argued.

He held up a breathing regulator.

"Ah. That explains the wet suit. And," I peered at him, "the oxygen tanks. You know those are really supposed to be yellow, but I guess that doesn't match the whole dark, mysterious merman prince aesthetic you have going on here."

"Did you call me a mermaid?" my not-rescue growled.

"Merman," I corrected. "But a prince. Like in a fantasy novel? You know, king of the watery shadow realm, the dashing man from the deep. But not any tentacles or anything like that." Shit. *Stop talking!* "Er...well, all that to say, I thought you needed saving. However, I was sorely misinformed."

I blew out a breath and ended up spraying the merman in the face with the water that was dripping from the wet hair plastered to my head.

The merman grimaced and wiped at his face.

"Sorry about that!" I reached out to brush off his face. Though mostly hidden by the black diving caul, his brow and nose were strong under my palm. I jerked my hand back.

It's sad because this is the most action you've had in the last eighteen months.

"Have a great day and enjoy this beautiful weather!" I croaked at him.

As I pivoted in the water, a man cleared his throat to my right. So as not to completely embarrass myself, I turned my yelp of surprise into a curse.

The new diver from the deep laughed, then several more men wearing black diving suits surfaced around me, all gray-eyed and strong jawed, though they seemed infinitely more amused than my non-drowning rescue.

"Did you make a friend?" one of the divers joked to the merman.

"Did you find my watch?" the mysterious merman shot back.

"I feel like since we're all brothers, you should forgive and forget."

The merman lunged at his brother in the water so quickly it was almost preternatural.

Dayum, he really is a prince of the shadow realm.

"I don't ever forgive and forget," the merman warned. "I will hold a grudge until the entire planet is a wasteland."

Then the merman let out a long, suffering sigh. "I will escort you to shore, ma'am."

"Bro, this will be the first date you've been on in years!" one of his brothers said with a laugh.

Merman turned on him, giving a slight flash of teeth. "And this is going to be your last day on Earth if you don't find my watch, Liam."

His brothers sighed and sank back down into the cold depths.

"I don't need an escort," I told the merman, feeling foolish.

"The water is freezing," he said, deep voice bouncing over the choppy waves. "You could pass out and drown, and then I will be blamed, and it will be a horrible inconvenience."

"It's cool and refreshing," I retorted.

"You aren't even shivering," he protested, following me as I did the breaststroke back to shore. "That means you're probably in the early stages of hypothermia."

"It takes a lot to make me cold," I said stubbornly. "This is nothing. I went swimming in Antarctica once. I petted a penguin. It was really cute."

Not as cute as you, Merman!

Shut up, brain!

But the prince of the shadow realm persisted in swimming silently next to me. Which was a problem because I was wearing... not much. Not to mention that I hadn't put on my nice underwear when I had left for my run—not that I owned any. The underwear I had on, I'd owned since high school. It had bunnies on it and holes in some inopportune places. And just because I didn't mind the cold didn't mean that my nipples didn't show it.

I paused at the metal pipes drilled into the side of the concrete embankment that served as a rudimentary ladder.

"Okay, so you showed me back," I said, starting to panic. I did not need him to see my terrible taste in undergarments.

"Do you need help?" Merman asked. Water droplets clung to his eyelashes.

I wished I could see his whole face.

I wish I could see the rest of him.

That thought did not help the nipple situation.

I blinked at him.

"Getting out?" He motioned.

"Nope," I said, continuing to tread water. I was annoyed to see he did it a lot easier than me. "Seriously, frog prince, you can leave."

"Ma'am, I think the cold has affected you more than you think," he said, jaw tense. "Let me take off my flippers and—"

"Cheater," I muttered.

"Excuse me?"

"You have flippers. That's cheating!" I said loudly.

His mouth fell open. "Cheating at what?"

"Swimming. Treading water."

"Are you going to get out, or am I going to have to drag you out?" he demanded.

"Don't touch me!" I shrieked.

"Then get out of the river on your own accord."

I continued to tread water. "Maybe I want to stay in a little longer."

The merman moved, the flippers giving him an unfair advantage, and grabbed me around the waist, his strong arms half hauling me out of the water.

I grabbed for a rung of the pipe ladder.

"Where are your clothes?" he said in horror.

"I was performing a rescue!" I yelled as I inelegantly hauled myself the few feet out of the water to land on the concrete walkway like a beached whale. "Time was of the essence."

"I fucking hate New York City," the diver said, shaking his head. "It's full of lunatics."

"Right back atcha, bud," I said as the river water dripped down my face.

CHAPTER 2
GREG

I hated most things. I hated networking mixers, price stickers on books that leave a residue when you remove them, and all the stupid names for the coffees at Starbucks. I also hated most people. If I didn't actively remind myself that I loved my brothers, I'd probably hate them, too, especially when they chewed noisily.

"It is not lunchtime," I snapped at Liam when I walked into my office to find my five brothers. "And people who lost my two-million-dollar, one-of-a-kind Patek Phillipe watch in the Hudson River then failed to find it should especially not be eating in my conference room in my tower at a time that is not a designated mealtime."

Liam stuffed the remaining quarter of his bagel sandwich in his mouth, jaw working furiously.

"I'm not eating," he said, bits of lettuce flying out of his mouth.

I'm going to have an aneurysm. Or a stroke. Or kill my brother.

"You should have taken that hot blonde girl on a date," Walker said.

"Did you get her number?" Carl drawled as I set my bag down.

I gave him my best glare. He gulped and sat up straighter.

"Care to try that again?" I asked.

"I have your coffee, boss," Carl mumbled.

"Why do we have to have a meeting on New Year's Day?" Beck complained.

"You could have stayed home in Harrogate," I reminded him, taking my seat at the head of the conference table. "In fact, you can go back there right now. Archer bought all our younger brothers ten thousand dollars' worth of fireworks for Christmas, and I'm sure you could be of use supervising the ensuing shit show."

"Hard pass! I don't really want to babysit," Liam said, leaning back in his chair and wiping the back of his mouth with his hand.

I loved my brothers. I really did. But, my god, they drove me crazy. It wasn't just their bad attitudes, lack of attention to things I considered important, or their terrible ideas, but also the fact that there were so goddamn many of them.

A by-product of a polygamist cult-leader father and his many wives, I had numerous half brothers, most of whom ran feral in the quaint small town of Harrogate a few hours away. My half brother Hunter did absolutely nothing to corral them, forcing me to trek out there on a biweekly basis just to keep some semblance of order.

The adults currently sitting around the table were my full brothers. Beck, the second oldest after me, was emotionally on a hair trigger and had inherited our father's explosive temper. Mike, the third oldest, would lie to my face that he was going to do something then turn around and just not do it. Walker, next in line, was capable of following directions when he felt like it, which was not often. Then came Liam, who back talked and considered himself creative. Sitting next to me was the youngest, Carl, who had no goddamn sense, and it was a miracle he could make it through the day.

"I would have thought you were on a date with the half-naked girl you pulled out of the water instead of sitting in this boring meeting," Liam said.

"Walker can track her down," Mike said with a snicker.

"No," I said. "Walker is supposed to be working on the collaboration with Svensson PharmaTech, not playing internet stalker matchmaker."

"Funny you should mention matchmaking," Liam said, sitting up. "I have your speed-date ticket here."

"You must have lost your mind if you think I am going on a speed date," I said flatly.

"But you have to." Beck gave me a slight smirk. "That's the only way to run into Martin Shaw."

"I've been monitoring his social media," Walker added, "just like you ordered. He's big into dating right now."

"No."

"But we haven't been able to score a meeting with him," Mike reminded me. "I have several new hotels for Greyson Hotel Group to build. I need him to invest his fund in the building costs. We can't just sit around waiting for him to finally decide to stop yacht shopping and to schedule a meeting with us. Everyone in Manhattan is going after his account. We need an in."

"If you don't, some other firm is going to swoop in and nab his investment," Beck said.

"I'll do it if you don't want to," Carl offered.

"Absolutely not," I barked. "Liam, send me those tickets. I'll have that contract signed this time next week."

CHAPTER 3
Belle

♡ ♡ ♡

"What are your New Year's resolutions?" Emma prodded thirty seconds after I walked into her teeny, tiny, micro, studio apartment.

"Make money," I said emphatically.

"I know, right?" Emma said breathlessly as she raced in a circle around the tiny apartment, picking up clothes off the bed then running to the oven, where she had a macaroni and cheese heating up, then to the freezer to chill the bottle of champagne I had brought.

"I got it on sale this morning," I said.

"You know I love anything on sale!" she said happily. "Oh shoot, can you grab the champagne flutes?"

She pointed. Her micro apartment was literally taller than it was wide. The ceilings were fifteen feet high, a vestige of the building's former use as a warehouse.

"A tall friend is super practical," Emma said with a giggle as I climbed on her step stool then easily reached up to grab the shoebox she directed me to.

"Why do you still keep these?" I asked her, handing her the box.

She petted it. "If I could afford a therapist, they would probably tell me that it's mentally unhealthy to keep the wedding goblets you stole from your lying, cheating ex's wedding to his lying, cheating co-cheater."

She handed me the goblet that read *groom*.

I looked at it and sighed. "It's ironic, you know. The guy at the wine store called me sir earlier."

"Oh!" Emma squeaked. "I'm sorry! You can have the bride glass."

"It's fine."

"He probably wasn't looking closely," she assured me, taking out the champagne bottle and pouring me a generous helping.

"You're a great catch," she told me earnestly as I drained the glass. "Guys like girls who can keep up with them drink wise."

"No, they don't," I replied. "They like delicate, petite princesses who eat half a hot dog and claim they're *so full*."

"Only if they have a spinning fetish," Emma replied with a snort into her champagne flute. "You know, they want to put her on their lap and spin her around!"

I rolled my eyes. "They certainly don't want you to jump in the freezing-cold water and rescue them in front of their friends and relatives."

"You have to tell me more about your watery prince of the deep!"

"Merman? Hopefully he'll drown the next time he's out there."

"It was a big moment," Emma said, digging into the cardboard box that she used as a coffee table. "He could be your prince come to rescue you."

"Doubtful."

"Was it big?" she asked, eyes wide.

I gave her a questioning look.

She pulled an entire chocolate cake out of her makeshift coffee table.

"You know, his shark fin." She pointed down to her crotch area.

"I didn't cop a feel! Besides, it was freezing cold."

"That's how you know if he's really packing or not. You should stalk him and then just randomly fling yourself in his path. Maybe he's rich!" she said in excitement.

I stood up to take the pasta out of the oven. "I don't think wealthy men go scuba diving early in the morning."

"Yeah, they do. That's eccentric rich." She cut a slice of cake for her and then one for me. "If he is, then you have to pretend to get hit by his limo, and then he'll take you back to his penthouse, and you'll live happily ever after. Even if he doesn't like you, at the very least you could still get a payout."

"Fairy-tale endings do not happen for large and tall girls," I said matter-of-factly. "We do our own rescuing."

Emma made an exaggerated pout. "That's not a good attitude to have at the speed-dating event."

"No, Emma."

"You have to!" she cried "It's a new year! Your resolution can be dating and getting back out there! You never had fun in high school—your parents never allowed you to do any extracurriculars, let alone date, because you had to take care of your brothers. This is your time to shine!"

"I'm fifteen years behind everyone else."

"So now we're playing catch-up!" Emma insisted.

"No one is going to want to date me. I'm too tall."

"Except…" Emma was gleeful as she pulled out a flyer. "I found you a dating event for tall people! You'll fit right in!"

I took the flyer from her. In spite of myself, I was intrigued. During high school and community college, I had always been jealous of the girls who always had a steady stream of boyfriends to choose from. They did fun things like go to the mall and hang out with friends, while I had to go straight home after class to take care of my brothers.

"Maybe I could actually find a boyfriend there," I said begrudgingly.

"Yesssss," Emma said, bumping my fist. "Now eat your mac 'n' cheese, then we're going to find something for you to wear."

• • • • • • • • • • • • •

"Am I at the right event?" I asked the woman at the table at the entrance to the hipster bar in Manhattan.

"You here for the tall-dating event?" she chirped then looked up at me, craning her neck. "Wow! You are really tall!"

"I thought that was the point." I tried not to sound annoyed as I looked around. I was the tallest girl there by quite a lot.

The hostess giggled. "This is actually an event meant for tall men," she clarified. "Not women."

"Oh." Feeling embarrassed, I fidgeted with my purse strap.

"But you can totally stay!" she said cheerfully, handing me my name tag. "Usually, all our tall girls are models and are obviously not going to come to a silly, little dating event!" The hostess handed me two drink tickets. "Have fun, and good luck!"

I almost wish she had told me to leave, I decided as I headed over to the bar to order a drink. Then I went to awkwardly wait for my drink near a petite girl flanked by two investment-banker types.

"Wow, you can really drink for someone your size," one guy said, obviously flirting with the girl. She let out a braying laugh, eating it up.

"I'm small, but I can drink like a fish and eat like a horse! Hahaha!"

Ahahahaha!!! Barf.

I know, I know. I sounded like a bitch, but honestly you could always tell when a short girl was in the room because she would always, always, without fail, make guys spend ten minutes guessing her height, then insist that the one-half inch mattered.

"Oh, let's play a game," Short Girl said, clapping her hands. "You guess my height, and then I'll guess yours!"

Here we go.

"Five even?" the investment bro with the red tie asked.

"Cloooseee!" Short Girl said, taking another sip of her drink.

I desperately wanted mine.

"Five one?" the blue-tied investment bro asked.

"Nope! Too high!" she said and gave a snorting laugh.

I shifted my weight.

The bartender set my drink on the counter. He gave me a frightened look when I went to pick it up.

"Thanks," I told him and handed him a dollar bill for a tip.

He gingerly took it from me.

"Then I guess six one!" Short Girl said to one of the investment bros as I walked past.

"You got it, girl!" he said happily.

I paused.

Just let it go.

But I was annoyed. I was annoyed at the merman. I was annoyed at the speed date. I was annoyed that the bartender had not put enough alcohol in my drink.

"He's not six one," I said, interrupting their little height jerk-off session.

"The hell?" Investment Bro yelled.

I turned. "You're not six one. I'm six feet tall, and you're shorter than me."

"You're wearing heels," he blustered.

"I assure you, I am not. I never wear heels." I gave him a toothy smile. "Men find it intimidating."

CHAPTER 4
GREG

I hate dating. I hate the ritual of it, the fake getting-to-know-you peacocking, the personality-less bars, the bland overpriced drinks. I never dated. In fact, I had sworn I wasn't ever going to marry. My father was on wife number eleven or twelve by now and was actively looking for the next one if rumors were correct. I had promised myself when I escaped the cult that I was not going to end up like him. And a big part of that promise was avoiding the endless courting rituals Leif Svensson loved so much.

"Hi!" The girl at the front desk looked up at me, eyes sparkling. "You might win the prize tonight!"

"Excuse me?" I said in a clipped tone.

The hostess giggled. Did she think I was flirting with her? I resisted the urge to make a cutting remark. I had eyes on my mark. I couldn't get thrown out before I had a chance to talk to Martin Shaw.

"There's a prize for the tallest guy here," she said with another giggle. "You're super tall; how tall are you?"

"Six five," I replied, trying to keep the annoyance out of my voice. I needed to get to Shaw.

"You're in the running." She held out two drink tickets. "Have fun!"

I pocketed them. They could be used for bribes if need be.

Shaw was across the room with his brother. I pushed my way through the crowd, ignoring the women who tugged at my bespoke suit, trying to entice me to talk to them.

I would need to have the suit dry-cleaned after this endeavor. This bar smelled like, well, a bar.

Shaw and his brother didn't seem all that happy to be there. They were angrily arguing with a tall woman with platinum-white hair.

"It's not my fault that you've been able to get away with lying for so long," she was saying, arms crossed.

Fuck. It was that girl—the crazy one from the river. Why the fuck was she here?

"Honestly? It's pathetic," she said.

"You're pathetic!" Martin's brother yelled at her. "You just get off on making men feel bad and laughing at them."

"Let's go, Todd!" Martin yanked his brother back then turned and left.

Fuck.

"What the hell is wrong with you?" I snarled at the tall woman. Her name tag read BELLE.

"Oh, did I insult a friend of yours?" she asked in a mocking tone.

"Why are you always in my business?" I snapped.

"Your business? I don't even know who you are." She glanced at my face then gazed into my eyes. Hers were an intense shade of blue, like the clear blue sky over a fresh snow.

"Oh my god! It's the merman prince!"

"Excuse me?"

She tamped down a smirk.

"I am not a mermaid man," I said, furious. "I am Greg Svensson of Svensson Investment with hundreds of billions under management. Don't you ever call me that again."

"Frog prince has an attitude," she said, mouth quirking.

"Or that." I snarled. I couldn't believe this woman. The Shaw account was worth twenty billion dollars, and she had quite possibly just lost it for me.

I took a breath. *Calm down. It's not over yet.*

"Why are you even here?"

"Same as you," she said.

Fuck, is she here after the Shaw contract?

But Belle took a sip of a toxic-looking blue drink that made me want to gag. "I'm here looking for a date."

Fuck dating.

"Don't turn up your nose," she said sarcastically. "This place is filled with the type of women you want."

"You have no idea what type of woman I want," I retorted.

"Please." She snorted. "You rich guys are all the same. You want a petite, slightly ditzy woman who is smart enough to be impressed when you use big, important investing terms like maturity distribution but will still laugh to her friends over drinks that she doesn't have a clue what her boyfriend does all day and doesn't care as long as he makes money."

She ended her tirade with one hand under her chin in a mocking Betty Boop gesture.

"That's not what I want in a woman."

"Of course it is." Belle downed the rest of the blue drink. "And I'll tell you why. It's because deep down," she pointed at me with the hand holding the glass, "deep down you and all the men like you are weirdos with mommy issues."

That hurt. My mom had abandoned me and my brothers when we were kids, leaving us to the violent whims of my father.

Fuck Belle. She doesn't know me.

"And all women like you," I spat back, "have daddy issues. You've been spoiled your whole life. I bet your dad bought you whatever you wanted, and now you're trying to find some idiot who will take over your bills."

"Fuck you. I rescued you yesterday."

"No, you didn't!" I practically shouted. "You literally did not."

Before I could make an acerbic retort, something tugged on my sleeve. I looked down.

"Oh my gooddd! You're, like, so tall!" a short girl squealed.

I looked back up at Belle.

She made a *ribbit* noise then blew me a kiss.

CHAPTER 5
Belle

♡ ♡ ♡

I should have known Greg was a Svensson. Multiple billions and multiple brothers—they were all the by-products of a polygamist doomsday cult. Their whole family had been in the tabloids lately. I had my own issues. I didn't need to add some asshat's emotional baggage to my load.

"Did you meet your Prince Charming?" Dana Holbrook asked me, one eyebrow raised, when I sat with her and Emma at a rickety café table the next morning.

"Just a frog prince."

Emma let out a squeal then clapped a hand over her mouth. "You saw him? Your king of the shadow realm?"

"He's not a king, just a fuckwit Svensson."

"Yes, but he's a billionaire fuckwit, which is even better than a merman king! Oh my god," Emma said, batting at my arm. "Use your super-duper hacking skills to find out where he lives, and then we'll stalk him, and you can jump in front of his car and live happily ever after."

Dana made a confused face. "I don't think that's how any of that works."

"It totally is!" Emma insisted.

"I'm not dating him," I argued. "I despise him. And he hates me."

"He's a Svensson brother," Dana said with an elegant shrug. "They're high-strung and histrionic."

"You're biased. You're a Holbrook," Emma said, taking a bite of her enormous cinnamon roll. "Your families hate each other."

"The Svenssons hate us," Dana said calmly. "We barely remember they exist."

"So no other tall men were there?"

"I didn't really stay to talk to any of them," I admitted. "I sort of insulted one guy, then I definitely insulted Greg. After that, all the other guys gave me a wide berth."

"Maybe group dates aren't your thing," Emma said. "Maybe you need to do some one-on-one dates. I started a Tinder profile for you." My friend wiped her hands and took out her laptop.

"I don't have time for dating. I need to either find a job or work on starting a company."

"We will get our investment firm off the ground," Dana promised. "That's why we're having the meeting today. Emma, you worked on Wall Street—"

"Yeah, before I got fired," she muttered, "unfairly because of my cheating, backstabbing ex."

Dana patted her hand. "That's why we are starting our own firm."

"I took a look at our assets," Emma said. "We really need to pull in more investors. We especially need a big client. The amount of cash we have right now is, in the eyes of Wall Street, basically nothing. Our current assets are as much money as those finance guys make just moving money around every hour."

"Top priority is to be on the lookout for more investors, ladies," Dana said.

"But first," Emma said, "we need to make Belle's Tinder profile!"

"Step aside," Dana said as Emma brought up a half-done Tinder profile on her laptop. "I work in media and advertising. This is my wheelhouse."

"Why is it about me?" I complained while Dana and Emma argued about what to put down for my hobbies. "Dana, why don't you go on Tinder?"

"My standards are too high for Tinder," she said. "Now Emma, we cannot use that picture of Belle. She looks like a hobgoblin."

• • • • • • • • • • • • •

The restaurant was crowded when I walked in that evening.

Emma: *Does he look like his picture?*
Belle: *Sort of?*
Dana: *To be fair, we lied about your height in your profile so…*

I sighed.

Eddie was sitting at a table by a large ficus plant. He seemed normal enough. He was wearing khaki pants and a polo shirt.

He stood up when I walked over. He was short—very short—with a mop of curly hair.

Don't judge people, I scolded myself. *You don't like being judged.*

Except I would judge Greg. I was still irritated at him. How dare he think my father had ever given me anything? Dr. David Frost hadn't given me anything I needed when I was a kid, let alone anything I wanted. I was the furthest thing from spoiled. How dare Greg think he knew anything about me!

Eddie nervously twisted his hands as I approached.

I shouldn't have let my friends lie about my height. Springing the fact that you're a six-foot woman on a guy on the first date was a risky move.

But Eddie didn't seem to mind. In fact, he seemed excited—a little too excited. He tugged at his pants as he stared up at me.

"Wow, you're even taller than I thought," he whispered.

"Erm…" I sat down, not wanting to loom in the middle of the restaurant.

"How tall are you?" he asked breathlessly.

"Five twelve." I grabbed a piece of bread out of the breadbasket. It had caramelized onions on top.

He blinked for a moment then giggled. "Six feet tall. *Six feet tall!*" He leaned forward over the table and licked his lips. "What shoe size do you wear?"

It's not the worst date ever. At least there are carbs.

CHAPTER 6
GREG

"**H**ow was the date?" Carl asked, bounding over to me when I walked back into the office the next afternoon.

"Unsuccessful."

"That's too bad," Carl said nervously.

He and Liam exchanged a look and surreptitiously tried to block me from going into my office.

I pushed Carl aside.

"Poor Greg didn't get laid."

I peered into my office.

A man with military-short blond hair and gray eyes framed by scars was sitting in my chair.

"How dare you show your face here, Crawford," I thundered.

My half brother just laughed. He was clad in his black leather motorcycle gear and had his dirty boots on my imported leather blotter from Italy.

"I didn't know you were shopping for the future Mrs. Svensson," he drawled. "You get more and more like our father every day."

"And yet you're the one who doesn't have a respectable job."

"You call scamming little old ladies respectable?"

"You have no idea what I do," I scoffed, taking off my overcoat and hanging it up. "Which isn't surprising since you disappeared right after we were kicked out of the compound."

"You can't still be holding that over me," he retorted.

"The rest of us sacrificed," I reminded him. "You left to be your own person or find yourself or whatever lie you told yourself to excuse abandoning your younger brothers."

"They don't seem too bent out of shape," he said, jerking his chin to the glass wall of my office, where my brothers gawked at him.

Crawford had been in the military since we'd been kicked out of the compound. He was in the special forces or some nonsense. He had never shown up for any family activity or holidays. Now here he was.

And I bet I knew why he had suddenly shown up.

I gave him a cold smile. "I think you're the one who is just like Dad. As I recall, he was only nice to you when he wanted something. And here you are, wanting to play happy family. What do you want?"

Crawford just leveled his gaze at me.

"Money? Influence? Connections?" I continued. "The answer is no, by the way."

"I don't want anything from you," Crawford said. "I already have an investor lined up—the Holbrooks."

"No," I said automatically. "They stole Hunter's and my first company. They are on my shit list."

One day Walter Holbrook will pay.

"Then make me a better offer."

"You think you're getting one over on me?" I asked him as he threw a packet with a proposal for a private security company at me.

"No, I think I'm getting money from you."

"Whatever." I threw the packet back to him without looking at it. "Go talk to Carl. I don't have time for such pettiness."

"It's not petty," Crawford growled. "We need an army to go after Dad."

"You mean like you did a few years ago?" I snarled at him. "When you not only failed to get rid of him but also made him more entrenched and more violent and made it more difficult to get accurate information about our sisters' whereabouts?"

"Next time I won't fail," he said stubbornly.

"Get out of my chair, and go talk to Carl."

"I'm going to have to have this chair sprayed down with bleach," I grumbled as I gingerly sat on the edge of it. I dusted off my blotter. Then I organized my pen cup, miniature globe, and pens in a linear arrangement.

I steepled my hands and forced myself to think. I needed to get close to Martin Shaw. Real estate development was starting to pick up in the city. I needed Martin's fund. I had my eye on several large swaths of land. Besides, I wanted to win. This was the account everyone in Manhattan wanted. It had to be mine.

I wrote a note to Walker to find out what dating event Martin would be attending next.

Of course I had absolutely no desire to attend. I was especially annoyed that Belle had wasted my time at the last event.

Honestly, who did she think she was? And how dare she accuse me of being shallow and having mommy issues? Actually, how dare she speak to me that way at all? No one spoke to me that way. My brothers certainly didn't, and on the few ill-conceived dates I had been on in my adult life, the women all had a certain deference toward me that Belle was sorely lacking.

Don't let her distract you.

But she was all I could think about. My mind wandered back to the "rescue" she had performed the other day.

"Lunacy. It's pure lunacy."

She had jumped into the slushy, ice-filled river water with no clothes on.

My mind supplied a crystal-clear image of Belle with her undergarments clinging to her curves.

"You're stressed," I told myself, rearranging my fountain pens again. "It's your family. You need a break."

Carl knocked on the glass door of my office.

"Go away," I told him when he opened it.

"I wanted to see how much you wanted to invest in Crawford's company."

My half brother grinned over Carl's shoulder.

"Carl," I snapped, "you have been working in Svensson Investment for years. Figure it out and use your good judgment."

• • • • • • • • • • • •

"Dinner's on me!" Crawford drawled as we arrived at the restaurant. "Since you gave me that very generous investment offer."

"I'm going to fire you, Carl," I told him.

"You said use my good judgment," my younger brother complained. "When Crawford goes to liberate the compound, he needs a whole army. That costs money."

"Crawford is not liberating anything." I pressed two fingers to the bridge of my nose. "I shouldn't have come to the restaurant."

"You always eat alone." Mike clicked his tongue. "It's not healthy, Greg. What if you choke on your steak and no one is there to save you?"

"It's a slippery slope eating by yourself," Crawford concurred. "Antisocial behavior."

"I'm around you imbeciles all day long. I don't want to spend all my mealtimes with you as well."

"But you do with your girlfriend?" Liam joked.

I opened my mouth to tell him off, but he just pointed.

There, like a recurring nightmare, was Belle. She was sitting alone at a table.

Crawford raised one scarred eyebrow. "Aren't you going to say hello?"

"Ask her if she wants to come join us!" Mike suggested.

"Yeah," Beck said, "since she was the one who has spoken to Martin Shaw the most, maybe she can give us some intel."

That made me angry all over again.

"Mace thinks she's stalking you." Carl held up his phone, where the messages on the group chat of all our brothers were coming in like a hail of bullets.

"Good news sure travels fast in this family," Crawford said with a smirk.

"Between your arrival and Greg's relationship troubles, no one has accomplished anything today," Mike said.

"Is she stalking me? What if she's some sort of Holbrook plant?" I said, staring at her.

"And I thought I was paranoid!" Crawford remarked. He smirked at me. "If you're not going to talk to her, I will. I've been overseas for the last two years. I could use a pick-me-up."

"Don't even think about it," I said automatically to oohs from my younger brothers.

"If I didn't have money invested in you all," I warned them, "I'd have you shipped to Madagascar."

I turned on my heel. I was going to figure out what the hell Belle was up to. After dealing with my father and his abuse and paranoia for my entire childhood, I didn't believe in coincidences. I didn't trust them, and I didn't trust Belle. I stalked toward her.

Focused on her food, she didn't look up.

"Why are you here?" I demanded. It was the same tone I used to keep my wayward brothers in line. But Belle didn't even flinch.

She neatly wiped her mouth and took a sip of her wine. "You're the one following me."

"No, I'm not!"

She looked up at me, blue eyes icy. "I was here first. I was at the dating event first. You showed up and started harassing me. That makes you the stalker."

"As if I would waste my time stalking someone like you!"

The tablecloth fluttered.

I glared at it.

A hand appeared from under the white fabric.

"What the hell?" Belle muttered, looking down.

Before she could move, I swooped down and grabbed the arm that the hand belonged to and hauled a man out from under the table.

"*You fucking creep*," I hissed, shaking him roughly.

He let out a scream like a rodent. "I'm here on a date. Don't hurt me!"

"Liar!"

"Tell him!" the creep sputtered. "Belle, please, he's going to kill me! I'm too young to die!"

"You said you dropped your fork, Eddie," she said, annoyed.

"I did!" he replied, nodding quickly.

"You seriously went on a date with this despicable specimen?" I asked Belle.

"Beggars can't be choosers," she said, taking another sip of wine.

"I will worship the ground your size-ten feet walk on," Eddie promised. "Just please don't let him throw me in a dumpster!"

I set him down. "Get out."

"But my dinner!" he whined.

"Out!"

He seemed extremely frightened by my tone and hauled ass out of the restaurant.

Belle pursed her mouth.

"So, no thank you?" I said after a moment.

"Thank you for what?"

"Rescuing you," I said.

"From Eddie?" she scoffed. "He was hardly a threat."

"He was under the table doing god knows what," I argued.

"I don't need your help," Belle shot back.

"Fine," I spat. "Next time you won't get it."

"There better not be a next time."

CHAPTER 7
Belle

♡ ♡ ♡

"You walked out? But that was your big moment!" Emma cried when I met up with her later in the evening.

I took a bite of the burger she had ordered for me. "As if."

"Greg came and rescued you from a terrible date," Emma insisted, waving a french fry around. "You should have let him buy you a drink, then buy you dinner, then take you around the city in his super-expensive car, then take you back to his swanky condo!"

"I don't want anything to do with someone like Greg."

"But he likes you," Emma pleaded.

"No, he doesn't."

"He does! That's why he keeps seeking you out. You have to go out with him."

"I'm already tired of dating, and I've only been on two dates," I said.

"Too bad because I have one more dating event planned for you," Emma insisted. "You can't give up yet. You at least need to work on your New Year's resolution for the first few weeks in January."

"This was not my New Year's resolution; it was the one you made for me," I reminded her.

Emma crossed her arms. "I told you to pick a New Year's resolution or one would be assigned to you."

• • • • • • • • • • • • • •

Even though I would never admit it to anyone, and even though I was having a hard time admitting it to myself, I had maybe actually been a little happy to have Greg show up and derail the date.

Not that I would ever tell him that, and not that I was happy in a romantic way. But the date hadn't been good. Right before Greg had shown up, I had been sitting there contemplating if I should just walk out or if I should make up some elaborate excuse about my nonexistent cat having an emergency.

Eddie had been way too strange. And he totally dropped that fork on purpose. If Greg hadn't shown up when he did, I would have kicked Eddie in the face for touching my shoe. Accidentally, of course.

But gosh, Greg had been so smug and sure of himself!

"Asshole," I muttered as I wrenched the door to the restaurant open the next afternoon.

My five brothers, seated around a table next to the window, looked up apprehensively as I stalked over to them.

I tried to tamp down my aggravation toward Greg as my younger brothers greeted me warily.

When the youngest had been in his senior year of high school, I had been at the end of my rope. Jack and Owen, my two oldest brothers, had started their own companies and were made of money. Had they helped me with our youngest siblings? No, of course not, because they had learned from our father that it was totally okay to be checked out of responsibilities that you didn't find appealing.

So, after I had done my sisterly duty and gotten Oliver into Harvard, I sold all of my belongings and went traveling. I hadn't told anyone I was leaving. I just disappeared. After raising five kids, I needed a break.

I was paying for it now. My abrupt absence had been a cannonball in my brothers' psyches, and now they all had made some sort of pact to make sure I never left again. It was annoying in that adorable, little-brother way.

"How are you, Belle?" Owen, the second oldest of my brothers, asked uncertainly. He stood up, but I grabbed the seat before he could pull it out for me.

Oliver used the distraction to reach over and steal a spear of pasta from Matt's plate.

"Stop touching my food!" Matt snarled.

"You ate some of mine!"

"Stop squabbling," I told them. They both slumped in their seats.

"They're heathens," Jonathan said, sliding a water over to me.

"You're a heathen," Jack retorted. "Belle, he moved into my condo, and now he's acting like he has tenant rights. I'm trying to live there with my girlfriend."

"You've been there since Christmas?" I asked Jonathan.

"My upstairs neighbor flooded her apartment," he complained.

"Get a hotel," Jack said.

"Hotels are gross," Jonathan retorted.

"You're so bougie," Matt teased.

"No, I'm not," Jonathan said. "You're bougie!"

I rolled my eyes. "Knock it off. Jonathan, get out of Jack's penthouse, and move in with Owen."

"No!" Owen said, horrified. The youngest two brothers cackled.

"It's not like Owen's bringing any girls back."

"Yeah, all he does is sit there like a sad sack!" Oliver added.

"You two are terrible," Owen said darkly, "and you wonder why Belle left."

Ugh.

"So," Jack said, twisting his straw wrapper in his fingers, "have you figured out if you're staying or not?"

My brothers all looked at me in concern. The skin around Jonathan's eyes was tight, and Matt and Oliver, the youngest, seemed visibly upset.

"Of course I'm staying," I said brusquely. "I have some business ventures in the works. Can't cut out now."

Jack let out an audible sigh of relief, and Owen patted me on the arm.

"I have, uh, money for your business venture, whatever it is," he said, pulling out a checkbook.

"And you can have a condo in my tower," Jack offered. "Where are you even living?"

"Crashing with a friend," I said, thinking of my sleeping bag in Emma's apartment.

"Stay at Jack or Owen's tower," Jonathan insisted. "Shit, why are you even working? Make them give you money. And then you can give some to me!"

"Yeah, Belle, seriously," Jack said, "we owe you big."

"And you need to live somewhere safe," Oliver insisted.

Da fuck?

"Look here," I told my brothers because I was nipping this in the bud right now. "I don't need you all to rescue me. I do the rescuing. I am the older sister. I don't want your money or your real-estate charity. I am perfectly fine."

"I just wish you would let us help you after all you've done," Owen said uncertainly.

"You're my little brothers," I said sternly. "I wasn't going to do anything less."

CHAPTER 8
GREG

I had just lain down on my couch and closed my eyes when the buzzer to the front door of my condo went off.

"We're here to help get you ready for your date!" Liam called out as he, Mike, and Walker breezed into my condo.

"Excuse me?" I swung my feet off the side of the couch.

"Your hate date."

"No."

"Dude, Martin Shaw is going to be there," Walker said.

"Look. He tweeted about it," Liam said, sticking his phone in my face. "He's super stoked. This can be your big bonding moment."

"You think the Holbrooks are going to be able to send anyone out there to the hate date?" Mike asked. "They're all shacked up. This is your big shot."

"Are the Holbrooks doing investing?" I asked, frowning. "I thought they did logistics."

"I heard rumors that one of them has been floating the idea of starting an investment firm," Walker said. "So if you want this contract with Shaw, you need to get out there with your dating game face on."

"Wear something nice," Liam said, holding up a paper bag from a high-end store. "Not your usual boring suit. You have to act like you want to be there finding Mrs. Right!"

He pulled out a silk shirt in a loud pattern.

"I refuse to wear that," I said flatly.

"You can't just roll up like you just left the office," Liam said. "Shaw is wearing something cool. You want to look cool, too, don't you?"

"At least change your tie," Mike coaxed.

"And wear a fun pocket square," Liam said, emptying the bag on the sofa. "If you really want to go all out, don't match them!"

• • • • • • • • • • • • •

"I look like a lunatic."

My brothers had given me a blue-and-silver tie covered in snowflakes and a pocket square covered in bunny rabbits wearing top hats. I inspected myself in the reflection of the bar window.

It's funny because Belle had bunnies on her panties.

"Absolutely not," I growled to myself, adjusting my tie. "Focus. We're here to seal the deal. Get in, get out."

Martin was across the room, talking to a pack of girls. I ordered one of the overpriced drinks from the bar then tried to figure out how I was going to insert myself into the conversation. My father had natural charisma, so much so that he could convince women to come live in the desert with him and his double-digit wives and feral children.

I didn't have that. I had his intelligence and steel will. But I was not made for the dating scene. If this contract wasn't so important, I would have made one of my brothers do this dirty work.

But Martin's face lit up when he saw me. He grinned.

"Dude! Where's your party outfit?" He motioned to his own colorful shirt.

Damn it. I should have worn what Liam brought. I was annoyed to know that my little brothers had been correct.

"Long day at the office," I told him ruefully. "I did wear a fun tie."

Martin pushed through the crowd of fawning women and inspected it. "Hmm. I'll allow it."

"I didn't mean to steal your date," I said, gesturing to the crowd of young women who tittered.

"This is the hate date," Martin explained. "You are supposed to note the woman you get along with the least who just grates on you. That signifies that you two will have passion in a potential relationship."

"Fascinating stuff," I lied.

"Unfortunately," Martin winked at the women, "all these ladies are fabulous."

They swooned.

I puked a little in my mouth. *I have investment pro formas I could be reviewing.*

"So," Martin said, throwing an arm around my shoulder, "you looking for love? I've seen you around on the dating circuit."

"It seems like it's time to settle down."

Martin nodded. "I have a relationship guru," he said. "Fantastic lady. She's helping me discover what kind of woman I need in my life. Not want, *need*."

"Is she?" I murmured.

"She can totally help you get in touch with your inner child," Martin said.

I had killed and buried my inner child.

"It's referral only," Martin whispered. "But I can put in a good word. You have to be totally on board with trying to find your soul mate, though."

"Absolutely," I said.

Martin looked at me expectantly.

I forced myself to dredge up whatever relationship drivel my half brother Gunnar would blather on about when he was telling me about the new show his crackpot production company was filming.

"I've been spending the last decade focused on growing my wealth," I said, "but I woke up one morning and realized, what's the point if I don't have anyone to share it with?"

Well, no one except my dozens of feral younger brothers who went through money like Coca-Cola.

Martin pressed a hand to my chest. "It's time. I feel it. You and I are the same person. Go forth and date, my friend. We will compare notes later this week."

I meandered around the room, making polite chitchat with the women there. My original plan had been to go home as soon as I talked to Martin, but he kept looking over to check on me. I couldn't just leave. I needed that hate-date meeting later in the week during which I would slip in the idea of Svensson Investment managing his fund.

"So did you find anyone you hated?" one bubbly short woman asked me.

"Everyone here has only been mildly annoying," I told her.

She let out a peal of laughter. "You're so funny!" Then she pouted. "I guess I don't hate you either."

"That's because you haven't spent any time around him," a woman drawled.

Speaking of people I hated—there, sauntering over from the bar, was Belle.

CHAPTER 9
Belle
♡ ♡ ♡

"Funny comment from someone who claims she's not stalking me," Greg sneered.

"Big, fighting words from a man with bunnies on his tie," I retorted.

"You had them on your underwear."

The words hung in the air between us like a cloud of steam. Greg seemed almost shocked they had come out of his mouth.

I narrowed my eyes at him. "You're just as bad as the foot-fetish guy."

"I didn't go seek out your underwear," he hissed. "You jumped into the cold water with no clothes on. You're some sort of exhibitionist."

"I told you, frog prince. I thought you needed rescuing."

"People like me don't need rescuing," he scoffed. "Little girls like you need rescuing."

He called me little!

My heart swooned. But my inner unshaved feminist raged at being called a girl.

"I am not some helpless girl," I snapped at Greg. It was a little strange to be yelling at a man who was taller than me. It wasn't often that anyone—man or woman—was.

He glared down at me.

"I raised my brothers, and now I'm starting my own business," I told him stubbornly.

"Adorable," Greg said snidely. "Are you selling candles? Homemade soap? Cupcakes?"

"It's an investment firm."

Greg barked out a laugh. "Investing is a man's game. You're going to be chewed up and spit out. Unless you're investing in, say, coffee shops, bakeries, or day cares or something."

"Asshole."

"Correct," he said. "I've worked in investing for years. You need to be cutthroat. Aggressive. That's not you."

"You don't even know me," I retorted.

"I do," Greg said, "You're out here looking for love, hoping to find a man who will complete you and be your soul mate. You have no intention of making your silly, little investment firm successful. Because deep down, you're looking for a man to take care of things for you. You want to skate by on your sexy body and your pretty eyes. You don't want to sacrifice."

He thinks I'm sexy!

Stop it! I scolded myself. *He just insulted you.*

But it was heady to have Greg Svensson compliment *me*. Even if it was followed by an insult.

"You're a jerk," I told him.

He let out a mocking laugh.

"See?" he said. "I knew you didn't have what it took. You can dish out insults, but you can't take it. You're not going to last anywhere near Wall Street."

"Are you all ready to mark down your hate date?" the event organizer chirped, handing each of us a mini pencil and a beige-colored card. "Just write down the top three people here you despise the most, and we'll organize dates with everyone!"

"I know who I hate here the most," I said, writing Greg's name down in all three spots.

"Rest assured, the feeling is mutual," he said.

CHAPTER 10
GREG

"That woman is insufferable," I snarled to myself the next morning.

I had a routine to make sure that I started my day off correctly. I awoke at precisely six a.m. Then I lifted weights and did cardio, then I ate three soft-boiled eggs and a bowl of oatmeal while I read *The Financial Times* and went over the day's schedule.

But instead of a relaxing morning during which I congratulated myself for the successful meeting with Martin Shaw last night, I kept spinning my conversation with Belle over and over in my head.

"An investment firm," I muttered as I reread the same paragraph of the financial-news article.

But Belle kept intruding in my thoughts.

It was aggravating because I did not obsess about women. Ever. That was what my father did, and I was nothing like him. And the fact that Belle was tall and blue-eyed with platinum-white hair? She was just my father's type.

"*Fuck*," I snarled, jumping up to pace around the open-concept kitchen and living area.

My email pinged with an incoming message as I was on my fourth lap around the room.

From: *The Hate Date*
Subject: *Congratulations! You have a match!*

As soon as I read that the organizers had matched me with Belle, I sent the email to the delete folder.

I didn't have time to date. And I certainly wasn't going to date Belle.

I resumed my pacing, becoming more and more aggravated.

What a stupid idea—a hate date. How can you start a good relationship by hating someone? It didn't even make any sense; nothing about dating made any sense! And Belle certainly didn't make any sense.

My phone went off, jarring me. "*What?*"

"Someone's grouchy in the morning."

"Mr. Shaw," I greeted my hopefully soon-to-be investor while silently cursing Belle for making me answer the phone so gruffly.

But Martin just laughed.

"Guess you're still hyped up on the hate date," he said. "I think it was one of the more successful dating events I've been to. How about you?"

"It was certainly unique," I said, grabbing my pen and starting to make notes about how to best mention my investment firm in our conversation.

"So did you match with anyone?"

"I did," I said with a sigh.

"Was she someone you hated?"

"Definitely."

"According to their website, hate sex is the best. And they say that's how you are supposed to turn hate into love. I was talking to some other guys who went the hate-date route and swear by it." Martin kept talking, but my hand had frozen while my brain short-circuited and latched onto the phrase hate fuck.

Belle.

Fuck.

Fuck.

I scratched out my notes.

"Seems plausible," I said.

"I'm trying to plan a really awesome date for my hate date," Martin said. "The website says you're supposed to plan things that pit you and your hate date against the world, like both of you having to do an obstacle course, learn a skill neither of you know, or go to see a play you both hate. It helps build camaraderie."

"Interesting philosophy."

"Did you set up a date with your match yet?" Martin asked.

"Uh, yes," I lied.

"So cool!" Martin said. "When is it? Mine is tonight. You and I totally need to get together and compare notes after."

"Mine is tonight too," I said in a rush. "I have a whole, big thing planned. Do you want to meet tomorrow and debrief?"

"Absolutely! Just send me a calendar invite! Take lots of pictures. I might need to steal your ideas."

I let out an uncharacteristic whoop after I ended the call. Martin Shaw's investment was almost mine.

Someone opened my front door, and several of my brothers ran inside.

"Oh thank god," Liam said when he saw me standing there. "We thought you had finally combusted from stress."

"What are you doing in my condo, and how did you even get inside?" I asked in annoyance. "This is the second time."

"Dude, it was an emergency!" Liam stated. "We were trying to save your life. You're welcome, by the way."

"Beck has key-card access to all the units," Mike said, pointing to our brother.

Beck gave a slight shrug. "I need to be able to access the units because some people have drinking problems."

"Not me," Liam said, pointing to himself. "I don't know why you're looking at me."

"Dude, you were completely wasted on New Year's."

"Everyone out!" I thundered. "I need to plan a date."

My brothers gaped.

"What?"

"With who?"

"Why?"

Mike held a hand to my forehead. "I think you might be running a fever. I'll have Parker send over some horse tranquilizers."

"Absolutely not." I swatted his hand away. "I am planning a date so that I have something to talk about with Martin Shaw at our meeting tomorrow," I said smugly.

Mike applauded. "That's why you're the boss. Way to seal the deal."

"It's not done yet," I cautioned. "I need to pull together a nice hate date and take pictures to discuss with him. You know, make it seem like he and I are on the same wavelength."

"Who are you asking out?" Beck said.

I grimaced. "Belle."

"Yikes."

"Can't go wrong with dinner and a boat ride," Liam suggested.

"That's too basic," Mike retorted.

"Besides, it's a hate date. I have to plan things that we both mutually hate," I explained.

"Poetry readings, art exhibits, charity dinners," Liam said as he listed off things that I did hate. But did Belle hate them too?

"I need some opposition research on her," I told my brothers.

"Already got you covered," Walker promised. "I had Crawford pull some info. I'll tell everyone to meet at the office in two hours."

• • • • • • • • • • • • • •

Crawford was smug when I walked into the conference room later that morning. "Look who's trying to pretend to be a human being and go on a date."

"Fuck off and go start your silly, little security firm."

"Please," he preened, "it's already started. I just landed a contract from the Richmond Brothers to do security at their next big fundraiser, and I'm about to sign a contract with Evan Harrington for the *Tech Biz* event."

Crawford clicked a button on his laptop, and a presentation popped up on the screen at the front of the conference room. "Belle Frost. Sister to Owen and Jack Frost, who you have done business with. So it looks like someone is eating where he sleeps."

"I don't care what Owen thinks," I scoffed. "And Jack is a moron. I need that Shaw contract. What are some of the things she hates?"

"The big thing is you, apparently," Crawford said. On the screen flashed a picture from the bullshit Christmas party Jack Frost had thrown a couple of weeks ago. There was me and Belle. She looked displeased.

"You're just the paradigm of Christmas cheer," Crawford said sarcastically.

"What else does she hate?"

"Her parents. Printers that have subscription ink plans. And the sun."

The next slide was a screenshot from a Swedish girl's Instagram. She was posing on the beach with a slightly sunburnt, scowling Belle, who was wearing a bikini. She looked fantastic in it.

"Belle has no social-media profiles, and according to the Frost brothers, she had been missing for the last two years."

"She was kidnapped?" I snarled, jumping up. "Who the hell did it?"

"Are you fucking serious, dude?" Crawford said. "I literally just showed you a picture of her on vacation."

"Right." I sat back down.

"According to her younger brother Jonathan, she doesn't like party planning, idiots, and food that is not served on a plate."

"It's incredible," I said, "you go to these restaurants, and they charge an arm and a leg, then they serve you your food on a piece of tree bark or a shovel."

"They truly are a match made in heaven," Beck remarked.

"I'm working up the perfect date itinerary," Liam said. "It's going to be the best hate date ever! What time is Belle free tonight? Because at seven there is a trust-fund kid doing a reading of his debut novel inspired by his three-month stint as an organic oregano farmer, and it sounds stupid as fuck."

"Uh…"

"You haven't even asked her yet?" Crawford raised one eyebrow that was bisected by a scar.

"It's not like she has anything else to do," I scoffed and dialed the number that had been sent with the hate-date email. The phone rang. And rang. "Shit."

"Send her a text message."

Greg: *Come have a hate date with me.*

"You can't send that!" Liam exclaimed over my shoulder.
"Too late."
But the text message bounced back.

Error: *Unable to send.*

"Fuck," I said. "I need to get in contact with her. I need to go on this date. Tonight. One of you—find her."

CHAPTER 11
Belle

♡ ♡ ♡

"He totally wanted to drag you back to his swanky penthouse and give you the best orgasm of your life," Emma said when I relayed the hate-date event happenings to her the next morning over brunch.

That was one thing I had missed while traveling—a good, old-fashioned American brunch with all-you-can-drink mimosas.

I topped off Emma's, Dana's, and my glass, then dug into my eggs Benedict.

"I don't think so," I told Emma. "He just seemed like he was aggravated that I was even there."

"If he had actually been annoyed, he would have left," Dana said. "Men like that don't sit around and do things they don't want to do. Trust me. I have quite a bit of experience with billionaires."

"He was totally flirting with you," Emma said. "Totally."

"He did say I had a sexy body," I admitted, feeling my face go hot.

"I was right!" Emma crowed then clapped a hand over her mouth when the people at the next table over gave her dirty looks.

"He totally likes you," Emma whispered. "You should subtly but not so subtly ask him out on a date."

"No," Dana said. "Male billionaires have fragile egos; they get intimidated easily. Also, they like the thrill of the chase. Emma, sign Belle up for another date. Then next time you see Greg at one of those awful dating functions, you can tell him all about your date. You have to egg him on, chum the water a bit."

She took a sip of her mimosa and wrinkled her nose. "Honestly, what does a girl have to do to get some vodka in here?"

• • • • • • • • • • • • • •

Belle: *My date still isn't here.*
Dana: *Figures. No decent guy wants to go on a date at six thirty in the evening. That's practically lunchtime.*
Emma: *It's just drinks! This is better. It's a no-pressure date.*
Belle: *Yeah. And there's that new romantic comedy on Netflix tonight.*
Emma: *I'm saving you a seat on my bed slash couch slash table!*
Belle: *We need to find somewhere else to move to.*
Dana: *After our investment firm is the top dog, you can move wherever you want.*

Emma: *Belle is going to be married by then.*
heart-eye emoji

I wasn't so sure about marriage to anyone, let alone Greg. My parents had a seemingly great marriage. Of course, it was at my and my brothers' expense.

Maybe it was better to be single. And besides, just because Greg was hot and tall didn't mean I needed to be fantasizing about marriage with him or even sex.

Bet it would be great.

I shivered, remembering how hard his body had been under the wet suit.

Down, girl.

I drained my glass and ordered another from the bartender, tilting my head down slightly so as not to freak him out like I had the last one. My dad liked to show me photos of Princess Diana. He would tell me how she always held her head down and looked up from under her eyelashes to disguise her height.

"And this is why men liked her," he would yell at me on one of the rare occasions he would pay me any attention.

I scowled after the bartender took my order. The position made my head hurt, and trying to look up with my head tilted down was giving me eyestrain.

"Belle?" a guy's voice cracked, and he cleared his throat. Guess my date had arrived. He slid onto the stool next to mine.

"Basil," I said, swiveling my barstool to face him and holding out a hand.

"It's actually not pronounced the British way," he said, shoulders slumping. "My mom literally named me basil like the plant."

"That's unique."

The bartender handed me my drink.

I straightened up. I wasn't going to be able to deal with Basil with a crook in my neck.

"I know something about crazy mothers," I assured him.

"I should have just changed it," he said and picked up the cocktail menu. "I mean, what is wrong with me? Why can't I just change my name? It's a few hundred dollars—I could just go down to the city hall and do it," he railed.

"It's probably hard," I said reassuringly. "You feel like your mom isn't going to love you if you change it."

"That's exactly what it is," he said, chin trembling. Then he burst into tears.

I patted Basil on the shoulder.

The bartender, wearing the stoic look of a man subjected to Saturday nights filled with inexperienced drinkers, wordlessly handed me a shot glass with brandy.

"Have a sip of that," I told my date.

"I just moved out of her house," Basil admitted, taking a handkerchief out of his pocket and blowing his nose. "It didn't go well. She's so controlling!"

"You have to live your own life," I told him.

"That's right." He downed his whole drink in one go then hiccupped. "I want to get laid."

"That's the spirit."

Then he lunged at me, throwing his arms around my neck. "Will you help me lose my virginity?"

"Whoa! Let's slow down." I stood up.

Basil was still clinging to my neck, and his feet were like eight inches off the floor when I stood up to my full height.

"Holy shit!" he squeaked, dropping to the floor. "You're so tall!"

"Yes, I've heard."

"I don't know if I'm ready for all of that," he said nervously.

The bartender handed him another drink.

"Your profile didn't say you were that tall." Basil downed his drink and swayed slightly. "What if I get lost in there?"

For fuck's sake.

"We are not having sex," I said loudly.

Basil burst into tears again. "Is it because I'm short?"

"No, it's because she has better prospects."

Ugh. The reply had come from Greg.

Ever since Emma had put the idea in my head, I was ashamed to admit I'd been fantasizing about Greg rescuing me from one of these terrible dates. Except the guy he was supposed to be rescuing me from was supposed to be big and burly. You know, more of a threat than poor Basil, who took one look at Greg, screamed, and literally ran out of the bar.

"Fancy seeing you here," Greg said.

Instead of hanging back and launching into a tirade about my stalking him, he reached out, settled a hand on my waist, and brushed a kiss on my cheek.

It was literally the most romantic thing that had ever happened to me.

I swooned.

Greg smiled.

Gosh, he was handsome!

Something is amiss! the rational part of me screamed over the destruction of the floodgates that had been holding back the desires of my inner teenage girl who had just wanted the popular boy to choose her!

Control yourself.

"I came to take you on a date," Greg said.

"What? Why?"

"We were matched by the hate date."

"I-I," I stammered. "B-but we don't like each other."

"That was the point."

I blinked. A guy, *a real guy*, wanted to take me out on a date?

"You didn't call me," I said, trying not to spin out.

"I tried," he said, leaning against the bar. "The number didn't go through."

"Right, it was a Google Voice number. Sorry about that," I said, still in shock over his simple statement that he had come to take me on a date.

Greg shrugged. "I found you anyway."

"How?" I narrowed my eyes. "Did you put a tracker on me?"

Greg laughed and leaned forward. "Better. I asked your brother Owen."

"Ugh. The last thing I need is my little brothers in my business."

Greg laughed.

It was the first time I had heard a real laugh from him. Low and deep, it rumbled like thunder. "Trust me when I say I completely understand."

"Yeah," I said, "as a Svensson, I bet you do."

He smiled. "So, the date—"

"Er, sorry, I forgot my jacket," Basil whispered from under Greg's arm.

Greg looked down at him.

Because he is tall! Greg is a very tall man! Taller than me!

Basil grabbed it off the hook under the bar then waved to me. "I had a nice time. We should have a repeat next week."

"Don't ever talk to her again," Greg said, frowning.

Basil gave him a little bow. "Yessir."

CHAPTER 12
GREG

Belle narrowed her eyes at me after her squirrelly-looking date scurried off. "What makes you think I'm just going to drop everything and go on a date with you?"

"You don't have anything better to do with your evening," I told her.

She puffed up in annoyance. "You don't know that! You don't know anything. You just came in here and interrupted me and—"

"Rescued you," I corrected. "I rescued you from yet another bad date."

"We were having a very enlightening conversation."

"He was literally crying in your arms," I reminded her, handing my credit card to the bartender to settle the bill.

"And you complained about my having 'mommy issues,' as you so eloquently put it, but that guy…" I shook my head.

"You would have spent your entire life picking up after him, calming him down, making him soup."

"And I wouldn't with you?" Belle crossed her arms.

I grinned at her. "Of course not. I offer you the life of a billionaire's wife. The only strenuous activity you have to do is figure out what to wear to your ladies-who-lunch date."

She stuck her tongue out at me. "Thanks, but no thanks." She grabbed her purse.

I wrapped my fingers around her upper arm before she could leave. "You can't run out before our date."

"I'm not going to be some billionaire's wife," Belle said tartly. "And if this is some sort of weird test, I don't have the time or the patience for it."

"It's not a test," I assured her, desperate to have the date. "We're matched, remember? I just want to take you out for a hate date. It could be fun."

"Anything that sounds like a hate date isn't going to be fun," she countered.

"Then it will be interesting at least," I said, escorting her out of the bar.

• • • • • • • • • • • • • •

"This is the worst presentation I've had to sit through since my brother Carl tried to convince me to invest in a small-rodent adoption app," I whispered to Belle.

"I think that would be cute!"

"Far from it. He uploaded a beta version to the app store. The only content consisted of people posting random pictures of subway rats they had found."

Belle snickered.

The girl in front of us in the audience turned around and angrily whispered, "Shhh!"

I clamped my mouth shut, and Belle and I both concentrated our attention on the stage, where a guy was reading from his debut novel.

"When he got home from the field, he went straight to a bar—*straight to a bar*—where they were playing pool. The women there, they glowed like the light from the environmentally friendly cayenne-powder bug bombs that had been his companions in the oregano trenches. One of the girls leaned over the pool table, her breasts like the perfect cantaloupes he had picked ten hours a day for a week last summer, veins running through them like a silver mine that his father used to work in, bouncing in time to the music from the jukebox."

"It sounds like that poor woman needs a doctor," Belle whispered to me. Her breath was slightly cool against my skin.

"And that guy sounds like he needs an editor."

"Niles is a fantastic author," the girl in front of us turned around to hiss, "and if you can't appreciate his genius, you can just leave. You are in the presence of greatness."

Belle looked at me, and I looked at her.

"I think I've had enough greatness," I told her.

She grabbed her bag.

"That was a terrible start to a hate date," she remarked when we were out on the sidewalk. "I mean, that guy was more pretentious than you, and you are insufferable."

"I am not anywhere near as terrible as that guy," I remarked as we walked along down the avenue.

"I don't know." Belle smirked. "You were pretty adamant about how you're some big-shot investor."

"That's just a fact, ma'am. I am a big-shot investor."

"I haven't seen you on the cover of a magazine," she countered, stopping short and spinning on her heel to face me.

"That's because..." I said, trying not to acknowledge that she was within kissing distance of me.

This is just for your investment. You're not actually supposed to be dating or liking her.

"That's because I am *actually* a powerful investor," I continued. "All these college grads, who are fresh out of their fourth-year economics class and have a cool million from their daddy, start a hedge fund and think they're hot shit. It's all marketing. They pay *Tech Biz* big bucks to be featured in their magazine. People like me, who have real power, who have real influence over investments in emerging market sectors, and who have a hand in shaping the very physical fabric of this city, prefer to remain behind the curtain."

I expected her to be awed, but she just tilted her head thoughtfully. "Interesting."

I didn't get the sense that she meant it in an offhand way, more like she was filing the information away.

"Picking my brain for your investment firm," I half joked.

"Maybe!" she said, winking and bumping me with her hip, putting me slightly off-balance.

"Oops," she said, grabbing my hand to steady me. "I grew up with five brothers. I'm too used to hitting first and hitting hard."

I could have dropped her hand, probably should have, but it fit so perfectly in mine.

"If you're letting your brothers roughhouse with you, you're a lot nicer than me," I said. "My half brother Hunter recently brought all the children into the city for a surprise visit, which he does occasionally whenever he's pissed off at me. They have absolutely no manners and always want to climb all over everything, including me and the furniture. I of course refuse to allow them to act like animals."

Belle laughed. It was like slipping into a hot bath.

"And I thought I had a lot of brothers," she remarked as I held open the door for her at the restaurant.

Belle looked around. "I'm begrudgingly impressed," she said, taking in the imported mahogany wood accents and the recessed lighting.

It was one of the hottest restaurants in town, for some reason.

"I thought this was supposed to be a hate date," she said after the server escorted us to our seats.

"Oh, you're going to hate it," I promised, grinning at her.

"Seems nice," she commented as a server placed a warm towel before each of us. They were folded into the shape of a rose.

Belle looked down at it and smiled.

"You know," she said, unfolding the towelette neatly. "The one and only time my parents took me and all of my brothers to one of the nice restaurants they frequented, my brother Jack thought this towelette was food. He stuffed the whole thing in his mouth and ate it."

I tipped back my head and laughed along with her.

"That's why I don't take my brothers to nice restaurants," I said, folding my own towelette neatly and placing it back on the little wooden tray. "They can't handle it."

"My parents were furious," Belle said. "Especially my dad. He had to take Jack to the emergency room."

"Oh, he *ate it*, ate it."

"Yep," Belle said. "I think he was just so nervous and wanted to make a good impression on our parents that he just wasn't thinking clearly."

Two servers came by with the first course and set it down in front of us.

"What is that?" Belle whispered, horrified.

We stared down at our respective pieces of tree bark.

I poked at the display with a fork. "I believe it is a pile of shredded parmesan with a stick and a chess pawn."

CHAPTER 13
Belle
♡ ♡ ♡

"Literally the only thing that arrived on a plate was the towelette," I ranted as Greg and I walked across town toward the water.

"What was more obnoxious was the tragic backstory that went along with each dish," Greg added.

"Totally," I agreed. "I had no desire to eat that soup after listening to the chef's story about how he invented it to commemorate his parents kicking him out of the house at age twenty-five."

"It certainly did taste sad," Greg said.

"Only because it was served out of an old boot," I said flatly.

Greg made a face. "For some reason, it was top of the best-new-places-to-eat list. At least I ordered the alcohol pairings."

"You really went all out for the hate date!" I teased.

"Anything for the person I hate the most," he said lightly.

"I hate to admit it, but maybe the hate-date people were onto something. It is nice that you and I hate the same things. Well, this one thing at least," I amended as we strolled along.

"What else do you hate?" Greg asked.

"It's petty," I said with a sigh.

"I live for petty grievances," he told me solemnly. "That's why I was out in the river with my brothers in the freezing-cold water. New Year's Eve, one of them crashed the yacht we borrowed while trying to race against a schooner and dropped my watch that he had borrowed, without asking, might I add. It wasn't even that expensive, only two million dollars. But I still made my brothers all go out there and look for it."

"Looking for a two-million-dollar watch is not petty," I said after my brain caught up to the fact that Greg had two million dollars to blow on a nice watch.

Greg shrugged. "All our time spent out in the water was technically more valuable than the watch, but I couldn't let my younger brothers get away with it. Otherwise, chaos will reign."

I laughed. "Yeah, you can't let little brothers develop bad habits."

"So what's your petty hatred?" he asked again.

"It's dumb," I said.

Greg stopped, pulling me toward him. "Tell me."

"Okay, so do you like Disney movies?"

"No."

I gave him a slight shove, but he pulled me back toward him. "Of course you don't," I retorted, looking up into his gray eyes. "That's why I despise you. Anyway, are you at least familiar with Cinderella?"

"Yes."

"Disney has a color for all their official princesses," I said, starting my rant. "There are some who wear traditional cultural garments, but the other girls all have a ball gown in a different color. Tiana has green, Belle has yellow, Cinderella has blue, and Sleeping Beauty has pink. Except," I railed, "in the movie, Cinderella's dress is *clearly* white. The only reason it looks blue is because the lighting during the nighttime dancing scene makes her dress blue, but it isn't! You know whose dress *is* blue, however?"

Greg's eyes were slightly widened.

Stop it, Belle. This isn't that important.

Except it was. Also the multiple courses had come with multiple glasses of wine, and I had drunk all the wine at dinner.

"Sleeping Beauty's dress is blue the entire movie! They should have made her dress blue and Cinderella's dress white as God intended." I let out an angry breath. "End rant."

"I don't think I've ever seen someone react that strongly about anything so petty," Greg said, a smile playing around his mouth. "It's adorable."

I felt a flush of happiness pass through me. Tall girls were never referred to as adorable. Ever.

"Do you want a cheeseburger?" I blurted out.

Greg raised an elegant eyebrow. "Is that some sort of sex thing?"

"Er, no," I said, a flush creeping up my chest. I pointed to a small burger place across the street at a corner. "It was a three-hour dinner, and yet somehow I'm starving."

The mouthwatering smell of french fries and smash burgers greeted us when we walked in.

"We're supposed to be doing things we hate," Greg reminded me.

"Oh, I am totally going to hate eating all this food," I promised him. Drunk me was a starving, bottomless pit. And I wanted everything on the menu.

"Can I have the number three with cheese fries," I read off the menu above the cash register. "And an order of mozzarella sticks, and a chocolate shake, please?"

What are you doing? I chastised myself as soon as the words came tumbling out of my mouth. *You can't just order all that shit and eat it in front of Greg. What is he going to think?*

But it was too late.

"You want anything?" I asked, ducking my head down slightly.

But Greg didn't seem fazed at all. "Yes, actually. All I've had to eat tonight were a pile of sticks, some dirty water, and that strange charcoal-covered onion bread. I'll have a number four. No shake."

The burger shop had seating outside with heat lamps, and we took our food out there.

"I love sitting outside in winter," I said happily as a few snowflakes fell. "More restaurants should do outdoor winter seating."

Greg sat down next to me on the bench and pulled me close to him. "You're not cold?"

"Nope."

His hand roamed around my back, lightly stroking me.

Inside I was elated. I could barely believe what was happening—Me! The tall, weird girl who the mean girls would make fun of in high school, and I was the one half lying on a hot billionaire's chest.

Calm down. Maybe he's just being nice.

Except that Greg's other hand had come up to cup my cheek.

"In the spirit of ending the date with things we don't hate..." Greg said, his deep voice rumbling through his chest. He tilted my head up. Then leaned down to press his mouth to mine.

The kiss was amazing! It was snow globes and champagne and New Year's Eve fireworks. He kissed me softly then harder, one hand cupping my face, the other on the back of my head angling me toward him.

The steam from our breath hung between us in the air when he pulled back.

"I thought you hated me," I croaked.

He gave me a rueful smile. "I do."

CHAPTER 14

GREG

What had possessed me to kiss Belle? She was merely a stepping stone to my acquisition of Martin Shaw's fund. Why in the ever-loving fuck was I trying to complicate things with her?

But I knew why. It was because Belle had looked so beautiful in the firelight. And the way she had rested against me? It felt like she belonged.

I pinched the bridge of my nose. "I must be losing my mind."

"Greg!" Martin called, walking into the VIP area of the restaurant at the base of Svensson Investment tower.

He sat down across from me, resting his elbows on the table. "How was the hate date?"

I smiled in spite of myself.

"My man!" Martin said, reaching over to clap me on the shoulder. "Pics, or it didn't happen."

I took out my phone.

I'd had the waiter at the fancy restaurant take a few photos of us, and then Belle had taken a selfie in the courtyard of the hamburger place.

"Nice, dude, she really digs you. Also, no fair on the super-fancy restaurant," Martin said.

"Both of us hate overly fanciful foods," I explained. "Besides, I am an investor. I can't completely drop the ball. I did need to impress her."

"What kind of investment do you do?" Martin asked as the server brought over two drinks.

Score.

• • • • • • • • • • • • • •

I was in a very good mood when I walked into the office after giving Martin the rundown of Svensson Investment's holdings. During lunch, I had tried to seem very casual with it and not pushy. I just needed to slip the idea in his head; I would follow up a few days later.

"Did you have a nice date?" My half brother Hunter said snidely when I walked into the conference room.

"You know what?" I said. "I'm so pleased about getting close to scoring a big investor that I don't even care that you just randomly showed up. You are not going to ruin my day."

"And here I thought you were happy because your date went well," Liam said.

"I thought it was a fake date," Hunter said with a scowl.

"It was a hate date," Carl said with a snort.

Hunter glared at him.

Carl backtracked. "You want a coffee, Greg?"

"You going to take her out again?" Mike asked.

"What? No," I said. "Of course not. It was a one-time thing to get Martin on my good side. You know, make him think we have something in common."

"The tangled lies my brother weaves," Hunter drawled.

"You're one to talk," I cut back at him, "considering how much shit we're in with Meg because of you."

Hunter's face screwed up. "Don't start that shit with me. What you're doing to Belle is way worse."

"I don't see how," I scoffed. "Even if it does go south, it's not like she's going to be mayor of New York or something. She's a nobody. This will never come back to bite us. My plan literally cannot fail."

But for all my promises that I was done with Belle, for some reason I couldn't keep my mind off her.

I kept thinking about how she had melted against me when I kissed her. I wanted to kiss her again. In fact, I wanted to do more than kiss her.

"And next on the agenda," Liam droned, "we're going to discuss moving all the children from Harrogate to Greg's condo. I will, of course, move in as the nanny."

"That's fine. Next item. Wait—"

"Great!" Hunter smirked. "I'll have Remy load them all up in the bus. They'll be over by nightfall. Fair warning, they have been doing the baking soda-and-vinegar volcanoes in their science classes, and several of them have become emotionally attached to their creations. I expect they'll be bringing them along."

Fuck.

"No, don't bring them here. In fact, the next time you do bring them here, you need to give fair warning. You can't just show up outside my door."

"If you would actually pull your own weigh—" Hunter began.

"I am the only one here making sure there is money in the bank," I snapped.

"Yeah, because you saddle me with taking care of all the kids."

"You were not employed at the time," I reminded Hunter. "All you were doing was running around town and every once in a while acting as a divorce lawyer. Get over yourself. Next item."

But my mind started to wander again as Mike gave a rundown of the new Greyson Hotel Group boutique hotel locations he was proposing.

If I were to take Belle on another date, not that I am, where should I take her? What would she enjoy and be impressed by?

Stop thinking about it. Belle is a distraction.

But really, if you thought about it, trying not to think about her was already a distraction, so the only logical thing to do was ask Belle for another date.

Satisfied that the decision was made, I turned my attention back to the meeting. Or tried to.

I wonder what she looks like when she comes.

CHAPTER 15
Belle
♡ ♡ ♡

"You know," Emma said at our meeting the next day, "the nice thing about being fired is that you can just go have tacos and margaritas at eleven in the morning, and no one's in the restaurant to judge you."

"I'm judging," Dana said as she poured the additional tequila shots she'd ordered into her margarita glass. "You can't order three of the same tacos. You need variety."

"But I love their fish tacos!" Emma pouted.

"Did Greg get a little fish taco yesterday?" Dana asked me slyly.

Curse my pale skin. I turned bright red.

"Did you sleep with him?" Emma squealed.

"No, I didn't sleep with him. We made out. Well, he kissed me in the courtyard outside the restaurant, then I stuffed a hamburger down my throat."

"You ate his meat?" Dana smirked.

"You gave him a blow job?" Emma inhaled a piece of her taco, and I whacked her on the back.

"You have way too much interest in my sex life."

"This is a big step for you," Emma insisted. "You're moving up in the world."

"You play your cards right," Dana said, "and you could have a ring on it in a year. Marriage to a billionaire. Not the worst gig ever."

"I'm not shackling myself to another man. I will be my own independent woman," I said firmly. "I don't want to end in another situation like I was with my father. I want my own money, my own company, my own power."

"Seize the castle!" Emma cried, jumping up and raising her margarita glass.

Dana smiled.

"I'm glad to see you're all in," I said. "Speaking of, how is the search for investors coming?"

"Belle's too busy drawing a map for Greg to find her clit to find any," Emma said loudly.

I cringed, but we were the only people in the restaurant drinking at eleven in the morning.

"And what about you who are unemployed and have Wall Street connections?" Dana prodded Emma.

"I have a few leads," she said, shoving the rest of her taco in her mouth.

I knew she would want another round soon, and I signaled the waiter for more.

"And more tequila," Dana said. "In fact, just bring the bottle."

"Loving our ladies-who-lunch moments," I said dryly.

"You need to be loose," Emma said, doing a shimmy as she navigated to a Word document on her tablet. "Investing is a creative endeavor. All the billionaire boys' club members always like to act as if it's based on math. And it is, but if you're trying to convince someone to invest in your fund, it's all about the personal connections."

She brought up a picture of a suspiciously familiar guy. "This is Martin Shaw. Martin and his douche brother are sitting on their late grandfather's money pile and are wanting to invest it. Word from a secretary I used to sneak out of the office and go get drinks with, he's supposedly looking for someone to manage his fund. His brother has been doing it but has not been getting great returns."

"There's no way we're going to convince him to invest with us," Dana said, topping off everyone's margaritas. "I was thinking smaller fish."

"No, we go after the big tuna," Emma said, banging her glass on the table.

"Uh, I think that might be a little difficult," I said after a moment. "Because I might have insulted his brother."

• • • • • • • • • • • • • •

I wasn't too upset that Martin wasn't going to be investing in our firm. I mean, what would we even say? We can totally get you a return on your investment. We have no office and day drink, but yeah totally trust us with your billions.

Not.

As much as Greg had bad-mouthed it, there actually was a lot of money in "girl businesses," as he so annoyingly put it.

Oprah was a billionaire. All the fitness and home-improvement shows were started by women. Women were the ones spending money. Shoot, Dana already had a star with

Romance Creative. We could build a whole investment firm around a niche market of catering to women with money.

I walked along to a quiet café to buy a green tea latte and a pastry when a man practically ran into me.

"Watch where you're going," I snapped reflexively.

"Still clumsy and clueless as ever, daughter?"

Fuck.

Dr. David Frost, aka my dad, aka a grade-A dick, gave me a flat stare.

You don't have to engage with him, I reminded myself. Just keep walking. He has no power over you.

But there was still a part of me that desperately craved my father's love and approval.

I took a deep breath. "Hey, Dad."

"Hey, Dad?" he said in a mocking tone. "You disappear for years, abandon your little brothers—we had no idea where you were, no one did—and then you show up in the city and don't even so much as come by for a visit."

"I've been busy," I said and pressed my lips together.

"Doing what?" my father sneered. "All you ever did was sit up in your room or babysit my sons."

Because that's all you allowed me to do.

But I kept my mouth shut. My father lived to argue. He was a world-famous surgeon with the ego to match. You couldn't win an argument with him—you would never change his mind, and you would never convince him to feel a shred of empathy toward you.

"I'm working on things," I said. "It's not anything that would interest you."

"Are you dating?" he demanded.

"Does it matter if I am?" I said, finally shaking myself out from whatever part of me still wanted his attention and turning to walk away.

My father took several long steps, catching up with me.

"You're too tall to find any man who's going to want you," he said sharply. "And you're not thin enough to be a model. Trust me, I went to school with the guys like the ones you're trying to date. It's not going to end well for you. Any man who is dating you is just doing it because he wants something."

I tried not to let him get to me.

"Come home, Belle," he said, tone wheedling. "You can have your old room back. You can take over the cooking, and maybe plant a garden. Your brothers hardly ever come visit."

"And you think they will when I'm around?"

My father flashed me one of his magazine-worthy smiles.

"Just consider it. Your mom and I miss you. We want you around."

• • • • • • • • • • • • •

Seeing my father had ruined my day and sent me into a tailspin.

"He didn't mean it," I tried to tell myself as I sat in the café staring at a blank page in my notebook. "He didn't miss me. He just wants me to be an unpaid housekeeper."

My stomach clenched. The thought of drinking my iced green tea latte was making me nauseous. I was so annoyed that my dad had ruined my afternoon.

When my phone buzzed, it was a welcome distraction.

Greg: *Want to go to the opera with me tonight?*

Belle: *Is this another hate date?*
Greg: *Oh thank god you hate the opera too.*
Belle: *Detest it. If I have to hear classical music, I only want baroque or earlier.*
Greg: *You are literally my dream woman. I have a better idea planned.*
Belle: *If it's a pretentious art-house movie in Swedish, I'm just going to tell you right now that's a no-go.*
Greg: *Like I said, woman of my dreams. I'll pick you up at your friend's apartment in a few hours.*

• • • • • • • • • • • • •

"You got a package! You got two packages, actually!" Emma was practically jumping up and down when I arrived back at her building.

"The wrapping paper is so pretty! And flowers. They're from Greg."

"He's taking me on a surprise date tonight."

"Oh my god!" Emma squealed.

I laughed and picked up the bouquet of flowers Greg had sent. No one had ever sent me flowers. Ever. Not so much as a dandelion. Now I had a huge bouquet of white lilies, peach carnations, and lush greenery.

"I know!" I said, letting myself swoon. I pressed my face into the flowers. "I need to dry this bouquet and preserve it forever."

"No, you need to give Greg a mind-bending orgasm, and then he'll send you flowers every day for the rest of your life."

I flopped down on Emma's narrow twin bed. "I can't believe he likes me."

"He's clearly an ass man," Emma said confidently, popping me with a towel.

I shrieked.

"Open the boxes! Open the boxes!" Emma begged.

I sat up, and Emma handed me the first of the big boxes. I undid the muted pink ribbon on it and carefully removed the lid, folding back the tissue paper. There was a note on top.

I wouldn't hate it if I saw you in this dress (or took you out of it.)

"Oh my god!" Emma squealed and clapped her hands.

I pulled the soft fabric out of the box. It was a navy-blue dress with a flowy, tea-length skirt.

"It's a princess dress," Emma said happily. "Try it on!"

As I slipped out of my jeans, my heart started beating. I was not a normal size. I had tons of issues finding clothes. Heck, a lot of times I gave up and bought from the men's department because that was the only place I could buy shirts that fit.

But the dress fit perfectly.

"He's a magical man," Emma breathed.

She had a full-length mirror that had some water damage and cracks in the corner. I stood in front of it and did a twirl. The dress flared out around me. "I'm never taking this off."

"You have to let me do something fancy with your hair," Emma said, clapping her hands. "We'll do a nice side chiffon, very feminine, with soft makeup."

"I don't know." I chewed on my lip.

"I spent my severance check on makeup," Emma said flatly. "I'm going to do your makeup. Now go take a shower and shave," she called as I slipped off the dress.

When I finally stepped out of the shower, I put the beautiful dress back on then headed to my duffle bag. I had a pair of super-comfortable leather ballerina flats. I felt like they made my feet look a little smaller.

Someone knocked on the door.

"Emma said you had a shoe emergency," Dana said when I opened it. "Nice dress." She held out a box to me.

"You're like some sort of day-drinking fairy godmother," I joked, taking it.

"Did you find nice shoes?" Emma asked Dana.

"Heels?" I said in horror, opening the box.

"Black goes with everything," Dana replied. "They're fuck-me heels. Every woman needs a pair—keeps the men on their toes."

"These are like four inches high," I said, appalled. "I would be almost as tall as Greg. No way."

"You're going to wear your ratty-ass flats that you dug out of a trash can?" She raised a perfectly sculpted eyebrow.

"I didn't dig them out of a trash can; I found them at the thrift store. They are my magic flats. They make my feet look smaller."

The flats had taken on a Sisterhood of the Traveling Pants level of mysticism with me. I had worn them for high school graduation—which my parents hadn't attended. I had worn them at community college graduation—that my parents had also not attended. And I had worn them on several job interviews—that my parents hadn't wanted me to go to.

Anytime I needed a confidence boost or there was a special occasion, I wore my flats. I had not been able to find another pair online. And I babied those shoes, only bringing them out when the situation absolutely called for it—like the date last night.

"I have to wear them out with Greg," I tried to explain.

"They do not go with that dress," Dana said, turning up her nose.

I petted my black flats. "Don't listen to her."

"You should wear your heels with it!" Emma insisted.

"Nooo, I'm already practically as tall as he is."

"He's not going to notice."

"Guys always notice," I replied, slipping on the flats.

"Open the other package. Open it!" Emma cried, shoving the box in my arms.

Dana and Emma watched expectantly as I undid the ribbon and removed the lid.

The note on top read, I know you say you don't get cold, but you may want this.

Inside the box was a beautiful silvery-gray fur cape.

"Wow," I breathed.

"You look like a fifties socialite," Emma said as Dana wrapped the coat around my shoulders. "You are so getting laid tonight."

"Not if she wears those ragamuffin flats," Dana said.

CHAPTER 16
GREG

Belle looked amazing when she walked out of the door of the slightly dilapidated 1920s Art Deco apartment building.

I brushed a tendril of her silvery hair away from her face then leaned down and kissed her.

"You look stunning," I murmured against her mouth.

"Thank you for the dress."

"That was for me to see you in," I growled, pulling her back in for another kiss. She wrapped her arms around my neck, pulling me down toward her. I kissed her hard there on the street, running my hands over the tantalizing curves of her body.

"We could just skip the date," I suggested, "and go upstairs."

Belle wrinkled her nose. I leaned down to press a light kiss to it.

"I live in my friend's micro apartment, and she's still up there."

"You go, girl!" someone yelled out of an open window. Belle rolled her eyes then waved.

"What's on that hate-date agenda for tonight?" she asked after I helped her into the limo.

"It's a non-hate date," I reminded her, pulling off the fur cloak. The halter top of the dress gave me clear access to her bare shoulders, and I pressed a kiss to her porcelain skin.

She turned her head to smile at me, and I claimed her mouth again. It was almost disturbing how quickly I had fallen for Belle. Or it would have been if it didn't feel so right to be with her.

"Champagne," I offered. "There's a charcuterie tray too."

I pressed a button and enjoyed the look of shock on Belle's face when the charcuterie tray popped out of a hidden compartment.

"You have a secret cheese compartment in your SUV limo?" She peered at me. "Are you sure you're Greg Svensson?"

"This isn't my limo," I told her.

"Whose is it?"

"It belongs to my investment firm," I amended, "but I did not authorize the customization of the limo. My brothers thought it would be fun to have. Apparently, stretch limos are not all that expensive, so I said, What the hell. Little did I know that they were going to spend hundreds of thousands of dollars customizing the darn thing."

"But you have a secret cheese compartment!" Belle snorted then fell against me laughing. "You should rent this out for bachelorette parties."

"Never. The whole thing would be covered in glitter."

I assembled a cheese cracker and handed it to her.

"No way," she said.

I was taken aback. "This is very fine imported cheese. I did not have this purchased at the bodega down the street."

"I'm not eating in this dress," Belle said, horrified. "I'm going to spill something on it."

"I'll buy you a new one."

"This is silk," she said stubbornly.

"You're not hungry? You don't want a drink?" I prodded then pressed another button that revealed a bottle of champagne.

"I do," she grumbled. "But I need a bib."

"What the hell? That's hardly romantic."

But Belle was already rummaging around in the limo pressing random buttons.

A drawer popped open, and a cascade of condoms fell out.

"Hoping to get lucky?" She winked at me.

"Those are not mine," I said.

"Safe sex is good sex," she quipped.

Don't think about sex with her.

"They're not my size."

"Not your size!" she crowed. "Look at you Mr. Biggus Dickus over there."

"I'm six feet five. Everything's bigger."

"And I'm sure all the girls spontaneously orgasm when you tell them your height," she purred.

"Did you?"

She narrowed her eyes at me then grabbed my tie. "You're going to have to work a little harder than that."

She released me and pressed another button. A full change of clothes, including a white dress shirt, unfolded from a side panel.

"This is why I don't give my brothers free rein over the funds anymore," I grumbled as she pulled on the shirt.

She smiled up at me.

My brain unhelpfully supplied a mental image of her in my condo, wearing nothing except one of my white dress shirts.

We are having a wholesome date.

But I wanted a more unwholesome variety.

• • • • • • • • • • • • • •

"Is this the famous yacht?" Belle asked when the limo pulled up at the harbor.

"No, that was a borrowed yacht that is now a yacht I have to pay for because my idiot brother wrecked it."

"So this is your personal yacht?" she asked as I led her up the gangway.

"I know this isn't supposed to be a hate date, but if for some reason your little investment fund makes billions on dog treats or whatever it is you're investing in, do not buy a yacht. They're money pits. You need to find a friend with a yacht. They are always desperate for you to use it so that they can justify their purchase to themselves."

"You think I'm investing in dog-treat companies?" she asked sharply.

I shrugged. "Seems like you could make a go of it. I can look over your investment numbers if you want."

"Oh, late nights at your office talking finance?" she teased.

"I have a billion-dollar view," I told her.

"Maybe I will need to come up and see it," she said, "when everyone's not there."

Shit, she was addicting.

"So are you going to give me the grand tour of the not-your-yacht?"

"Did you want to see the bedroom?"

Her eyes widened suddenly.

Too fast.

"You should see it," I said, keeping my tone conversational though all I wanted was to take her down there and take off her dress.

"The Richmond brother who ordered this yacht has absolutely zero taste. He spent the first twelve years of his life literally locked in a house with his half brothers, and apparently he passed the time drawing up a ridiculous yacht, and when he made his billions..." I said as I guided Belle down the hallway to the master bedroom and flung open the door.

"He decorated the whole place in a Pokémon theme!" she finished my sentence, laughing.

"He told me he regretted it immediately." I closed the door then wrapped an arm around her waist.

The yacht was in motion. I didn't want her to fall. I also wanted to feel her pressed against me.

I led her out to one of the upper decks, where the crew had laid out a nice spread.

"There are a number of options," I said. "Though I did request hot food since there is quite a chill tonight."

"And what if I want a different option?"

CHAPTER 17
Belle

♡ ♡ ♡

As soon as we left the bedroom, I was kicking myself. What if that had been my only chance to get laid this year? It was pretty obvious Greg wanted to sleep with me. Right?

I wished I could ask Emma or Dana for advice. But I wasn't about to take out my phone. Besides, Greg was real and right there in front of me.

"I can have anything you want brought here," Greg assured me.

Ugh. Stupid, literal, finance dude.

Before I could lose my nerve, I stepped up to him and grabbed the lapels of his jacket. "I just want something that isn't on the table."

Catching my drift, Greg smiled then leaned down—yes, down because he was taller than me!!!—and hungrily claimed my mouth.

It was a fantastic kiss, better than the last two. His hands slowly traced up my dress, under the fur coat, then around to cup my breasts through the thin silk.

I moaned against his lips as his tongue slipped into my mouth, his hands roaming lower and lower. I gasped, breaking away from him.

"There are other bedrooms on this yacht besides the one bedecked in Pokémon," he said in that deliciously deep voice.

"I'm not picky," I said, hardly daring to believe I was even considering it. I blinked then looked over his shoulder as motion caught my eye.

I peered.

Was that…

Greg turned right as a huge humpback whale flung itself out of the water.

I shrieked, "A whale! In the harbor!"

I jumped up and down and grabbed his arm. "Did you see that?"

Greg grinned at my reaction. "The water's cleaner now, so there have been sightings."

"I can't believe there's a whale in New York Harbor! Best date ever! Nothing will ever top this," I gushed.

I laced my fingers around his neck and kissed him.

"Though maybe if we were on your personal yacht…" I teased.

"Never."

• • • • • • • • • • • • •

"How was your evening?" Owen asked cautiously when he walked into the café where we were meeting.

"What makes you ask?" I replied, narrowing my eyes at him. Though I'd had several fantastic evenings with Greg, my younger brother had meddled in my love life, and I wasn't going to let that slide.

Owen shifted his weight. "I, uh, just thought you seemed happy." He looked at me warily.

"I may or may not be happy." I clamped down a smile.

"Greg better be treating you right," Jack said loudly, coming over to the table.

"Jack!" Owen barked. "Look, Belle, I didn't mean to—" he said in a rush.

"I know exactly what you did," I told him. "You were playing matchmaker like some eighty-year-old Greek grandmother."

"I just thought you and Greg might have some things in common," Owen said defensively. "But I was right, right? You do seem happier."

"Greg sure is happy," Jack said, taking the seat to the right of Greg. "The Svensson brothers are over the moon! They said he's the most pleasant he's ever been."

"Beck is concerned," Owen said. "Apparently Greg floated the idea of buying a yacht."

"A yacht!" I said. "Good gracious."

• • • • • • • • • • • • • •

Belle: *Are you sick?*
Greg: *No?*
Belle: *I heard a rumor you were going to buy a yacht.*
Greg: *...*
Greg: *It's a good thing I'm not running a mob or some sort of top-secret operation. My*

brothers can't keep their fucking mouths shut.

Belle: *You can't buy a yacht.*

Greg: *I mean, I could.*

Belle: *It's a terrible idea.*

Greg: *I know. You're distracting me and making me irrational.*

Belle: *Maybe I better come over there and give you a blow job to stave off the impulse yacht buying.*

Greg: *I'd rather eat you out if you're offering.*

"And you just didn't respond?" Emma shrieked when she read through the messages.

"What do I say to that?"

"You started it," Dana remarked, pointing to the phone with the hand holding her martini glass.

"I know," I moaned. "What do I even say? Yes? Should I come over at seven or eight? Do you prefer waxed or au naturel? Oh shit! I need to wax."

"Pro tip," Dana said. "Shave. You have very fair skin, and I foresee wax ending redly and badly."

"Oh my god." I clapped my hands to my cheeks. "I can't possibly do this. Maybe we should just go get pizza."

"You have to respond," Emma said, shaking me.

"Send him a topless photo," Dana said, standing up to mix another vodka tonic.

"I don't think my boobs are nice enough for a topless photo," I replied, looking down at my chest.

Dana picked up the chilled vodka bottle. "Take off your shirt," she ordered.

"What?"

"Hurry up. I have dinner with my brothers tonight, god help me. This is the foolproof method for a boob shot."

I gingerly removed my shirt then my sports bra.

Dana poked me in the chest with the freezing cold bottle.

"Shit," I cursed.

Dana took a sip of her drink.

"Now just play with one," she said, picking up my phone.

I awkwardly put my hand under my boob. "This feels weird."

"Yes, because you look like you're giving yourself a mammogram."

"Pretend like you're doing a Playboy shoot," Emma coached. "Cross your arms and just let one nipple sort of peek around." She manipulated my arms.

"Back arched, shoulders back, hips forward," Dana instructed.

I felt like a wooden puppet with my limbs all twisted.

"My back hurts," I complained while Dana took the photos.

She sniffed as I put my shirt back on. "These pictures are serviceable." She scrolled through them and showed me.

"I can't send him these!"

Except I sort of wanted to.

Dana shrugged. "If you want him super excited, you can. Or you can just show up to his office tonight and be like, 'Wanna fuck?' I'm sure either way, he'll take you up on your offer."

CHAPTER 18

GREG

"So this is where the magic happens!" Martin said when I met him in the lobby of Svensson Investment tower. "Bet you impress all your dates with this place."

"I don't exactly bring them here."

"What? A tower would totally impress your hate date, I bet! Just casually bring her by on your second date and be like, Oh yeah, this is just my tower. No big deal."

"We already had our second date," I admitted.

"My man!" Martin punched me lightly on the shoulder.

I smirked and extended my arm, gesturing him to the elevator.

"You know," Martin said, "I had been thinking about going all in on investing and building my own tower, but then I remembered that I like the finer things in life. I need low stress, a nice girlfriend, and I'd love some kids. It seems like it's hard to have that when trying to manage an investment company."

"You can always have someone manage your funds for you," I suggested, trying to sound casual.

Martin grinned. "That's what I was thinking. It's just so hard finding someone trustworthy who isn't in it for themselves."

"You need to look for a fund that's not managed by just one person ruling over it like a feudal lord. You need a fund that has checks and balances and collaboration. You also want a fund where the people in charge don't just think of you like a walking stack of money but take your own desires and value into consideration when finding industries and companies to invest in."

Martin was nodding along as I spoke.

"Totally," he said as the elevator opened up on my office floor. "I'm going to talk to my spiritual advisor first, though. I might just give it all away to build dog-rescue centers. I'll see what the tarot cards say."

I forced myself to keep a straight face.

"But," Martin said as we walked into my glass-enclosed office, "I'm not here today to talk about me. I'm here to talk about you. What do you have planned for your third date?"

"Not sure," I said as my phone went off with an incoming text message. I ignored it. "What do you have planned for yours?"

"Mine didn't pan out," Martin said with a sigh. "But my dating guru suggested trying something a little more out there like a farming date. She thinks I need to get more physical, so I'm dating this horse girl. You know, you and I should double date. Well, triple date. My brother has a new girl he's dating. She's super into Christmas, though. Like it's nonstop Christmas carols. She has multiple Christmas trees in her house with the whole getup."

My phone went off again.

"That her?" Martin asked craftily.

I picked up the phone, glanced at it, then immediately slammed it down on the table.

"Guess so!" he said, standing up. "I'll leave you to it. Triple date this Friday, don't forget!"

I should have walked Martin out, should have sealed the deal, but instead I just nodded. As soon as he left, I looked again at the picture on my phone.

Was that Belle?

Of course it is, idiot. It's from her number.

The topless picture was… hot.

If my office wasn't walled off in glass, I might have even considered jerking off to it.

"Did you have a stroke?" Beck demanded from the doorway.

I jumped, my phone clattering to the table. I snatched it up. "I'm fine."

"Carl said you've just been sitting there for the last five minutes, and I just saw our big potential client wandering around in the lobby whispering to the plants," Beck continued.

"I'm fine," I growled at him.

Beck was not convinced. "I'm telling Hunter he needs to come into town. You're not acting like yourself. You were even nice to the secretary this morning."

"Out of my office!" I barked.

I went back to my phone.

How to respond?

But my brothers were staring at me through the window. I couldn't compose a coherent message, let alone process the picture with them glued to the glass like that. I grabbed my coat.

"I have a meeting," I told my brothers. "And stop standing around gawking. Get back to work."

"Can we bring the kids into town for a pizza party?" Liam asked me from his spot sprawled on the couch.

"Fine," I said.

"He really is nicer," Carl whispered.

• • • • • • • • • • • • • •

I was losing my edge and losing my mind. How had this woman, who I barely knew and had spent sixty percent of the time I had known her hating her, started to occupy so much of my mental headspace?

Even now, instead of working on the best way to make my case to Martin that he should work with my firm, I was being driven to Belle's apartment. I didn't even know if she was going to be there.

I stared out the window at the stone and brick buildings of the historic neighborhood.

Just tell the driver to turn around. This is nuts. You've lost it.

Except there walking along the sidewalk, big bag slung over her bare shoulder, was Belle.

"Stop the car," I said to the driver, opening the door before the SUV had come to a complete stop.

Belle froze then went into a fighter's stance and pulled a foot-long metal flashlight out of her bag, brandishing it.

"Holy shit!" I exclaimed, holding up my arms.

She relaxed when she saw it was me.

I approached her warily.

"Are you just looking for a fight?" I asked incredulously.

"Do you always creep around in an SUV and jump out acting like you're about to kidnap someone?" Belle retorted.

I grabbed her purse strap, pulling her toward me.

"You can't just send someone a picture like that and not expect drastic action to be taken," I said in a low voice.

"You act like that's a rare occurrence," she said, blue eyes bright in the sunlight. "I'm sure you have tons of women sending you topless photos."

"I assure you, I do not. I'm a respectable business owner. I can't have lewd photos all over my phone," I said, leaning in. "It's a terrible distraction."

I brushed my lips against hers then kissed her harder. Her mouth was delicious, but I wanted more. "Come with me."

"I need to go to a meeting," she said. Her skin was flushed, though, and she was breathing hard. "And my train is almost here."

"I'll give you a ride."

CHAPTER 19
Belle

♡ ♡ ♡

Yeah, I need a ride on that D.

As if he was reading my mind, Greg leaned in to kiss a hot trail down my neck. The press of his lips against my skin made me feel shivery. His hands came up under my skirt to stroke me through my panties.

You can't have sex in the back of a limo. What if the driver hears? It would be a new low for you.

I pushed Greg off and cast a glance at the glass dividing us from the driver.

"You can't see him, and he can't see us," Greg said, jerking his chin to indicate the darkened glass barrier separating us from the driver.

"But the driver could still hear us," I countered.

Greg's smile was wicked. "Then you had better keep it down." One hand rose to cup my breast, the thumb pressing over my nipple. "You can do that, can't you?"

Could I? It had been a while since I'd had sex, and even then it hadn't been all that great. I had hardly been brought to screaming ecstasy, but something told me that it might be a little difficult to keep my mouth shut with Greg. But my body still craved him.

I deserve this. I've had a hard few years.

I twisted around, my legs over his lap. He caught me around the waist and brought our lips together. The kiss was as searing as it was dirty. His tongue flicked against my own teasingly. I let out a little gasp of air that didn't go farther than between us.

He shifted again, laying me down, his body pressing over my own. I was a tall girl and rarely felt safe and cocooned. Greg managed it without effort.

We kissed, my hands rising to clutch at the lapels of his jacket. His own hand slid over my knee, up my thigh, and inward.

"Greg," I whispered as his fingers found home. I was already hot and wet for him. When the tips of his fingers brushed against my pussy lips, I felt another slick gush.

His eyes sparkled—part mischief, part admiration. "That's what I like to see," he murmured, kissing my neck. One hand kneaded at my breast, the other moved up and down my pussy, stroking me. "I want a taste of you."

I groaned and immediately slapped my hand over my mouth to stop the sound. Greg met my horrified look with a devilish smile.

But he was waiting for my answer. I nodded. Hell yeah, I had wanted to ride that dick to see where it took me, but suddenly I wanted that tongue on my pussy even more.

I all but shoved him down.

Greg went with a chuckle, sliding down to the floorboard with surprising grace. He shoved my knees apart, making me nice and open for him.

I leaned back, praying to every god that I knew of that we didn't get in a car accident or make a hard stop. Talk about awkward moments.

Greg's fingers slipped under my skirt again and hooked the hem of my panties. He removed them in one slow slide. Once they slipped off one foot, he placed a kiss to one knee then the other. His eyes met my own one last time.

Somehow, I was able to cock an eyebrow at him. "You did promise me a ride."

"I'm a man of my word," he agreed and, still grinning, ducked his head under my skirt.

The first swipe of his tongue against my pussy had me biting my lower lip to keep back the noise. He spread me with his fingers, and his tongue slid gently over my clit. I shivered from head to toe, pressing back against the seat, canting my hips up to give him a better angle. More... I needed more...

A low whine escaped my throat. I felt his chuckle, deep and rumbly, up through my core. Greg set to work, swiping again and again over my clit—pausing only to swirl around it to give me just that much more sensation.

His fingers joined the party, dipping in and out of my entrance.

My breathing came in harsh pants. I wanted to yell out my pleasure. I didn't dare. Instead, I covered my mouth to keep the little sounds down. My free hand tangled in his hair, tightening to let him know I was close.

He redoubled his efforts, and for a moment, I was in complete bliss. My climax rushed toward me, pleasure coiling tighter and tighter... until I came, groaning. Greg licked me through until the last of the waves receded.

I was still breathing hard when the car pulled up at the restaurant.

Greg smirked as I staggered out of the car. "Have a productive meeting."

• • • • • • • • • • • • • •

"You made it on time, after all," Emma said. "I thought you were going to be late. We already ordered for you." She pointed to a large bowl of creamy mushroom pasta.

"I, um, got a ride." I sat down across from my friends and put down my bag.

Did I ever!

"From who?" Emma asked. "It wasn't the landlord, was it? He's a creep."

"It was Greg."

I grabbed the ice water at my place setting and downed it. Just thinking about him *down there* doing *that* with his tongue was making me overheat.

"Looks like you had the ride of your life," Dana remarked.

"It wasn't like that."

"So you're just sexually frustrated he didn't get you off?"

I looked around askance at the crowd in the restaurant. I didn't need people hearing about my formerly nonexistent now way-too-exciting sex life.

"I mean, he did..."

"While he was driving?" Emma gasped.

"He had a limo."

"You did it in front of the limo driver!" Dana toasted me with her drink.

"I got carried away," I groaned.

"I'll say, if you were having a tumble in the back seat!"

"He kept his clothes on."

"You didn't even give him a reciprocal blow job?" Emma asked, stabbing her fork at me.

"I was trying not to be late for this meeting," I said, digging into the pasta. "Crap, I'm famished. I didn't realize a good orgasm could make me so hungry."

"You totally need to bang Greg," Emma insisted. "This could be your one shot at true love."

"Absolutely," Dana added. "He's way better than all the other guys you dated. They didn't even pay for dinner."

"To be fair, Greg kept showing up and ruining my other dates," I said, eating another bite of pasta.

"He's totally into you if he's being that territorial," Dana said emphatically.

"Seal the deal! Seal the deal!" Emma chanted. "Maybe he'll buy you an apartment."

I made a face.

"I promise I'm looking for one," I told her. "I've just been trying to figure out our investment angle. Since we have Romance Creative, maybe we could position our firm as specializing in media investment and offbeat real estate development that will appeal to women and therefore the guys who want to be around them."

"Sounds good to me," Dana said. "Of course, the main thing is we need capital."

Emma slurped up a bite of her pasta. "You both have rich brothers. Can't you just ask them for a loan?"

"Absolutely not," I said forcefully. "I have spent the last twenty-odd years being beholden to my father. I will not be reliant on men for money ever again. We are running this investment firm, and we will bootstrap it if we have to. Sweat, blood, and tears, ladies. You don't need to marry men to become billionaires."

"You're just going to be reliant on them for sex, right?" Emma said with a giggle.

CHAPTER 20

GREG

I must be going crazy.

In fact, I knew I was going crazy.

The feel of Belle, her legs wrapped around me, her hot, wet pussy bucking against me—I just wanted to bury my cock in her.

My phone went off like it had been doing the last couple of hours. My brothers were texting me, wanting to know where I was, could I look at stock spreads for those tech companies, did I want to contribute to their dumb start-up idea. I didn't have the bandwidth to think about any of that, let alone compose a coherent response.

Belle was taking a long time in her meeting. I had thought that it would be short—maybe an hour since the meeting had occurred at lunchtime. However, I'd been sitting in the car for over two hours, and she was still in the restaurant having an animated conversation with her friends.

Probably talking about the latest episode of whatever show girls like, I decided.

The smart thing would be to tell the driver to take me back to the office. The even smarter thing would have been telling him that two hours ago.

I pressed the intercom button.

"I'm going to be right back," I told him. "Going to get some air."

I headed down the block to a café. I would purchase a coffee and see if Belle was anywhere close to wrapping up. If so, I was totally going to take her back to my condo and fuck her brains out. If not, I would go back to the office like a normal person.

"My man!"

"Good afternoon, Martin."

"You here to pick up your hate date?" he joked. "I saw you walking her to the restaurant a few hours ago. My brother and I grabbed lunch at the place next door."

"Yes, I had another meeting," I lied, "then came back over here. She doesn't seem to be done yet."

"Chicks always love to talk," he said as he poured three packets of sugar into his paper coffee cup. "You should see my current girlfriend. I bet she and Belle will talk nonstop on Friday."

"That's the girl you're bringing on the date?" Martin's brother frowned.

"Is that a problem?" I asked, more sharply than I intended.

"She's so tall," he said, mouth twisted.

"You dated that model, Todd," Martin reminded him.

"I guess. But that girl Belle is just mean," Todd complained.

"Why? Because she called you out for lying about your height?" I said before I could stop myself.

Fuck. Wrong thing to say.

Martin's brother reared back. "She didn't have any right to do that! She should have minded her own business."

"Just calm down!" Martin pushed himself between Todd and me.

"Whatever. I'm out of here," Martin's brother said, turning and leaving the café.

"It's not you. He's mad about the investment," Martin confessed.

"What's wrong?" I asked, still worried I had just blown the deal.

"My dad gave me control of the fund after he passed away since I am older," Martin explained. "Todd doesn't get a vote until he's thirty, and he's super salty about it."

"So are you going to wait until then to find a fund manager?" I asked cautiously. My plans had assumed that the Shaw money was coming in now, not in four years.

"Naw," he said. "My spiritual advisor insists that I need to have the money managed now. She said it's bad for my chakras to be constantly concerned about it."

"I'm glad to help in any way I can," I said smoothly.

"We'll talk on the triple date," Martin said cheerfully, clapping me on the arm. "I gotta go calm down my brother."

I smiled. "Yes, I have younger brothers myself. They are a handful!"

Score and crisis averted.

I felt smug as I ordered my coffee. Martin and I had a natural connection—he seemed to trust me, and he had said we would talk about the investment on the triple date coming up.

That account would be mine.

I was probably going to get laid.

Life was good.

It would be even better, of course, if Belle would get out of her meeting.

She was still there when I peeked in from across the street.

She was also still there when it was dark out and the streetlights had come on. I had officially been sitting in front of the restaurant for hours. Instead of using the time to be productive, I had gone through in my head all the ways I wanted to fuck her.

I looked out the window again.

Just leave.

She has to be almost done. You've already wasted an entire day here.

It's the sunk-cost fallacy.

But finally Belle and her friends were paying the waiter.

I had the driver pull around to park in front of the restaurant. I checked my reflection in the window and stepped out of the car, hoping I didn't look like someone who had been sitting in a parked limo on the street all afternoon.

"Greg!" Belle exclaimed when she walked out of the restaurant, waving goodbye to her friends. "Perfect timing!" She smiled up at me. "How did you know I was here?"

Instead of trying to come up with a plausible lie, I swept her into my arms, kissing her hard.

"I'm an investor," I growled, nipping her bottom lip. "My timing is impeccable."

"Guess what, Mr. Big Shot Investor?" she said, running her fingers up my tie. "I was talking about investing too."

I kissed her once more then opened the car door for her.

"Really? For five hours?" I asked.

"We had a lot to cover."

"Did you decide between investing in fashion or cupcakes?" I joked, fully intending to give her an appetizer before we went back to my apartment for the main course.

But Belle pulled back from me, obviously pissed. "You think my company is a joke, don't you?"

"No," I lied. "But you have to start small. No one is going to trust you with, say, a ten-billion-dollar fund until you've shown you're able to not lose it all in a bloodbath. I mean, you don't even have an office. You met your partners in a restaurant."

"Part of what we were discussing was renting office space," she said primly.

"I could just give you some office space," I said, frowning. "I own a whole tower, after all."

"I don't need your charity." She crossed her arms.

"You don't even want to come look at it?" I crooned. "It has a killer view."

"I bet you really impress all your dates," Belle said.

"And my investment clients."

CHAPTER 21
Belle
♡ ♡ ♡

Greg was an asshole. He was handsome and sexy but still an asshole.

"You know," I said, cutting Greg off mid-explanation of high-school-level basics of investing. "I think I like you a lot better when your mouth is in my pussy and not mansplaining investing to me."

"I'm just trying to help," Greg said as I followed him through his now-empty office floor with only the emergency lighting giving off a low glow of light.

"I know how to do investing," I snapped at him. "I made hundreds of thousands off Bitcoin."

"Bitcoin isn't investing," he said haughtily. "It's just gambling. Real investing is something like real estate or series A funding for a new technology company. By the time you're trading stocks, you're a small fish."

I followed him into his corner office and let the glass door slam behind me.

He moved to the wet bar at the side of the room.

"You're just so full of yourself. You think you're so great."

"Of course I'm great," he said, pouring each of us a drink. "I have an eighty-thousand-dollar bottle of scotch at the bar in the corner office of the tower that I own with a view of all the other property in Manhattan I've developed and the companies I've invested in. I don't just think I'm 'so great.' I know I'm 'so great.' And I'm trying to give you the advice that normally I would be paid six figures to give at a conference keynote. You can't just show up on Wall Street with a plucky attitude and good intentions. You need to be intelligent, ruthless, and single-minded."

He regarded me thoughtfully. "You're cute, but I'm not even sure you have it in you, to be honest. I'm trying to save you from yourself."

"God, I hate you sometimes," I seethed, even though part of me was ecstatic to be called cute.

Greg didn't seem fazed at all. He just smirked and removed his suit jacket. "Then I guess I'm not going to make love to you in my condo as I had originally planned."

Wait, no sex! my brain screamed.

"Instead," Greg continued, sticking two fingers down the front of my shirt, "I'm just going to hate fuck you in my office."

My brain seemed to freeze at his words and then kicked into high gear along with the rapid pounding of my heart. I swallowed as Greg stepped right into my space, pulling me into a kiss. It was aggressive and demanding.

The fingers he had slipped down my shirt curved around my right breast and squeezed, making me moan.

He pulled at the buttons of my shirt, snapping a couple as much as unfastening them. I let him walk me backward until my butt hit the edge of his desk. He pressed me farther back, pinning me down and kissing me. Both sides of my shirt came away, my bra-clad breasts open to the air. He cupped me over my bra, pulling away from my mouth to kiss and lick at my clavicle. All I could do was thread my fingers through the back of his hair and try to hold on for dear life.

"Greg," I groaned, delighting in the fact that I could make noise this time. Not too much, but some.

"You're wearing too many clothes," he growled.

I sat up and shrugged the rest of my blouse away before I reached back to unclasp my bra, finally freeing my tits.

He fell on me again, kissing and sucking, taking first one nipple into his mouth and then the other. I arched my back, giving him access. Somehow, my own fingers worked at the buttons of his shirt. I managed three buttons before he pulled away, shrugged off his clothes, and tossed them away. When I reached for his pants, he gripped my wrist, stopping me with a smile.

"Ladies first," he said, then stepped back, still holding my arm to pull me to my feet. Then he turned me around to the desk.

Oh yes, I yelled inside, and maybe on the outside too. His hands came up and gripped my ass, squeezing me through my skirt.

"I love your ass," he murmured, and then his hand slid lower, sliding up my skirt to run along the edge of my panties. "I love the taste of you." He unzipped the skirt then pushed it down to pool on the floor.

His voice was rough, and his hand was even rougher, stroking me insistently through the thin fabric of my panties. I moaned, bucking back against him.

He made a growling sound of approval and yanked downward, rolling my panties over my hips and down. Then he pushed me over the desk and spread my legs wide. I was wet and aching for him.

"You going to give me your cock?" I panted.

"I don't think so."

I looked back to see that his knees had hit the floor. Then I let out a cry when Greg pressed his face against my pussy. His tongue dipped in to swirl around my entrance, one finger reaching up front to press and circle around my clit.

I moaned, clenching my hands against the slick surface of the desk. I was wet, and his tongue only made me wetter. I pushed back against his face, his fingers, hearing low groans come out of my throat as if I were outside myself.

Greg spun me higher and higher, until I knew that I was moments from peaking.

"Greg, I'm going to…"

I felt him smile against me as the orgasm crashed over me.

It left me sweaty and panting against the desk, the mahogany against my overheated skin.

The air shifted as Greg moved behind me.

"I thought you were going to give me a hate fuck," I slurred.

Greg paused for a moment, then I heard a dark chuckle. He gripped my hips, fingers digging into my ass. I was immediately wet and aching for him.

Greg pressed the bulge of his cock up against me. His fingers tight on my ass, he forced my legs wider. He rubbed his bare cock against my pussy as I tried to grind back against him.

"You want this?" he said in that deep voice. "You want me to hate fuck you over my desk that cost more than the assets you have under management?"

"Yes," I moaned, my fingers clawing at the imported leather blotter on the desk.

I heard the crinkle of a condom wrapper.

One of Greg's hands left my ass to rub my pussy as he put on the condom.

"Give it to me," I begged. I was sloppy wet from my arousal and his attention.

Greg grabbed my ass again then thrust inside me, filling me as he forced me to take every thick inch of him.

"Oh..." I clenched, tightening reflexively.

"Fuck, you're so tight, Belle," Greg said, voice rough.

He pulled out, pushed in again with a long thrust, and...

"Fuck," he said as he buried himself in me again.

My pussy tightened around him, my whole body shivering with desire. I loved how his cock fit perfectly inside me. His next thrust took me up to my toes, and I let out a long moan. Pleasure curled up inside me.

"You like that," he observed, cock hitting the same place with every harsh thrust. "Let me hear you."

"Yes... Greg, yes. Give me more!"

"Good." With that, he gripped my hips and began to fuck into me like he was going to make me his.

I moaned, one hand holding on to the edge of the desk, the other clenched in a helpless claw. The point of every one of his thrusts hit right up against that secret spot in me, taking me from hazy to needy so fast that my head spun.

I was a far cry from the cool, calm boss bitch I wanted to be. Greg completely owned me. I moaned out my pleasure and scrabbled for leverage to shove myself back on his thick cock.

Greg changed speed, thrusts going from long and deep to fast and brutal. Forehead braced on the desk, I rose again to my tiptoes, all but biting my lips to keep from shrieking my pleasure.

"That's it." The hitch in his voice told me he was nearly as gone as I was. "Come for me."

I crested for a second time, hanging onto the desk for dear life.

Greg followed mere seconds later, pounding me as I cried out his name.

When he stilled, Greg pulled me upright and wrapped his strong arms around me, pressing kisses to my face.

"I really like you, Belle," he said, voice rough. "Stay with me. Forget your investment scheme. Let me take care of you. I can keep you safe and make you happy."

I really wanted to say yes. I wanted to finally be rescued. I wanted the happily ever after with Greg. But I knew I would never forgive myself for being a sellout.

CHAPTER 22

GREG

I wanted last night again and again for the rest of my life. Being in her, arguing with her, fucking her—Belle was all I needed in my life.

I had wanted to bring her back to my condo for another round, but she insisted I take her home.

"I can buy you a place to live," I offered.

"I don't need your handouts," she said, hand paused on the car door.

"It's not a handout," I protested. "Really, it's a selfish decision on my part. If you have your own apartment, I can come by and fuck you whenever I want."

Belle gasped as I tangled my fingers in her hair, pulled her head back, and kissed her.

"Like right now," I growled against her mouth.

She moaned against me.

"You have a thing against sex in the limo, which I respect, but if we were in front of your swanky *pied-à-terre* and not your roommate's closet, we could go upstairs and I could eat you out then fuck you all night."

She spread her legs slightly, and I used the opportunity to stroke her through her panties.

I felt her shiver in my arms, and she tilted her head back, giving me access. Giving me permission.

I kissed her hard, my stroking fingers increasing both pressure and speed, running up and down the length of her pussy.

She shifted, widening her legs a little more, completely wanton. As a reward, I shoved the fabric of her panties aside to let my fingers get direct access to play.

She groaned, biting her lip.

"No," I said. "None of that. Don't hide your pleasure from me."

Belle's next low moan was full-throated and immensely gratifying to hear. My finger found her clit, and I moved a fingertip over it with gentle, teasing motions.

My eyes were locked on her face, watching for every pleasured reaction.

"Greg," she whispered, "I hate it when you tease me."

I smirked. "Funny, because I love it." I leaned forward to whisper in her ear. "And I really love it when you beg for me."

Belle whimpered as I brushed her clit ever so softly. "Please… Please… I want to come."

"That's what I like to hear," I said and let my lips fall over her again, kissing her as I shifted my hand, thumb now pressing over her clit while my index finger gently teased in and out of her wet hole.

Her next inhale was a shudder, and she gripped my shoulders, rocking her hips up to increase her pleasure.

"Greg, more..."

I gave her exactly what she wanted, adding another finger and plunging into her deep.

"Oh! Oh!" Her eyes half shut in bliss, she moved with my hands in a slow, sensual rhythm. One hand came up to cup her own breast, her lips parted. "I'm close..."

In answer, I increased my pressure on her clit, pumping my fingers in and out of her in a frantic rhythm. Distantly, I could feel how hard I was, getting this beautiful woman off. But all of my attention was on her—my own needs secondary.

Belle inhaled sharply and then, with a gasping cry, climaxed.

I fingered her through it, wringing out every bit of sensation I could until finally she gripped my wrist and pushed me away, panting.

"You can't tell me you don't want my cock after that," I told her.

I kissed her flushed cheeks then her mouth, red from biting her lips to keep from screaming.

"But unfortunately it will have to wait for tomorrow."

I'd helped her out of the car and watched as she'd walked into the apartment building in a daze.

Yes, I decided. *I need her in my life forever. In fact, I think I might marry her.*

• • • • • • • • • • • • •

"I'm sorry. You're going to marry this chick you only just met?"

"I didn't say I had any concrete plans," I told Crawford. "But you asked me how it was going, and I said that I could see it ending in marriage."

"I thought you were just using her to get the Shaw contract?"

"No point in wasting a good thing," I said matter-of-factly.

"Is that where you were all yesterday?" Beck demanded. "I had to rearrange my whole schedule because you were MIA and missed a meeting."

"I see you survived," I said.

"Hey, Greg's back!" Liam stuck his head in my office. "Hunter said he's dropping the kids off tomorrow evening."

"No, I have a date."

"You have had a date with Belle three nights this week," Walker remarked. "You must really like this chick. I don't think you willingly have gone out of your way to spend three consecutive nights with anyone."

"It wasn't consecutive," I growled. "And I cannot supervise the kids. I need to take Belle to the date with Martin and his brothers. I can feel it; he's close to making a decision on the firm. He thinks we're good friends, practically."

"I thought Belle was starting an investment firm," Beck said with a frown. "That's what Owen was saying. You sure you want to take her around our big star client?"

"She's going to be investing in things like bakeries or pet-clothing companies," I said offhandedly. "It's not like she's a real threat. Now get out of my office. I need to prep for the date and the big pitch to Martin and his brother."

Though the post-sex clarity from last night was enough to get me through organizing my pitch, the fact that I was trying to work at the desk where I had fucked Belle not even eighteen hours before was quickly wearing down my concentration.

> **Greg:** *You busy?*
> **Belle:** *Why, are you begging for a quickie?*
> **Greg:** *I just want to see you.*
> **Belle:** *You are totally incapable of working at the desk we just fucked at! *laughing, crying face**
> **Greg:** *I may need to just buy a new one.*
> **Belle:** *I'll make you fuck me on that one too and ruin your concentration.*
> **Greg:** *I want to hate fuck you.*
> **Belle:** *How about lunch first?*

• • • • • • • • • • • • • •

Belle was typing away at her laptop when I walked into the restaurant.

"I thought you said you leased an office?"

"Start of next month," she said happily, jumping up to wrap her arms around my neck and kiss me.

I would never tire of being greeted like that.

"And I am so ready to not work at café tables," she continued. "The chairs are super uncomfortable, and I have to buy a drink or food every hour or so."

She packed up her stuff.

"You don't want to stay here?"

"I've been staring at these same four walls all morning, and I need a change of scenery," she explained.

"Let's go to the brasserie down the street. They have German food like schnitzel, and they have *weisswurst* on Sundays for brunch, which we totally should go to. They also have awesome *currywurst* and french fries, which is what I'm ordering."

I smirked. "Guess I wasn't the only one distracted today."

"This is an innocent desire to eat good German sausage," Belle insisted. "I totally haven't been thinking about sucking on your dick all morning."

CHAPTER 23
Belle
♡ ♡ ♡

I was satisfied to see Greg stumble slightly at my comment about sucking his dick. Which I did want. Especially since I only had a glimpse of it last night before he was ramming it in me.

"You know," I said, wrapping an arm around his waist then letting it go lower to brush his ass that you could bounce a quarter off, "I might actually be convinced to have sex in the limo."

"That's who you found?"

I looked up to see who asked the question, expecting it to be one of the local crazies. Instead, it was my mother walking toward me arm in arm with my father.

Greg could not meet them. My parents were awful on a good day. My mother still believed that I owed her for all the sacrifices she had made and never failed to remind me that I was an ungrateful daughter. I had sworn when I left two years ago that I'd have no contact with her, yet here she was.

I tried to turn Greg to jaywalk, but my parents were already upon us.

"Really, Belle," my mother said, turning up her nose. "You can't date him. You'll have freakishly tall children."

"It's fine if they're boys," my father interjected.

"Excuse me, do you know these people?" Greg asked me, drawing himself up to his full height and glaring down his perfectly straight nose at my parents.

"She's our daughter," my father said, adjusting the immaculate white lab coat he was wearing over his suit.

"Is she paying you?" my mother asked Greg. "You're paying him, aren't you? To pretend to be your boyfriend."

"Mom," I hissed. "Stop it. Please."

"She's right," my father said, piling it on. "He's too handsome for you."

My father turned his attention to Greg. "My practice partner has a very pretty daughter. She's not quite as tall as Belle, but she is a bit thinner."

I wanted to sink into the pavement. When my father went on a rant, there was never a way to stop him. He just kept talking until he ran out of steam, then expected you to thank him for the privilege of listening to an insulting asshole.

"He was just with me at the press conference about a case we're doing. We operated on that basketball player who was in the swimming accident. You know, the one on the news," my father said. "Anyways, this girl is great. She did all these extracurriculars in high school, even went to study abroad in France then attended Johns Hopkins and breezed right through. Now she's a doctor. Belle barely graduated high school and of course went to a community college, so it's not like it was that difficult, but she still only barely passed. You could do so much better."

"Huh," Greg said, the slight exposure of one of his canine teeth the only indication he was about to go into full-asshole mode. "Personally, I find it amazing she was actually able to graduate considering that she had to take care of her five younger brothers and two mentally ill parents."

"I beg your pardon!" my mother sputtered.

"Why else would you have your teenage daughter raise your five younger sons?" Greg drawled. "It's the logical conclusion. My father, who is, quote, 'mentally unstable,' and my mother, who has the emotional maturity of a five-year-old hyped up on sugar, were also terrible parents. I had to raise my younger brothers, so I am of course sympathetic to Belle's plight."

"I have two PhDs!" my mother said shrilly.

"Aww, did Belle print those out for you on the computer?" Greg said mockingly. "Did you get to use your favorite crayons to color them?"

"Asshole!" my mother yelled at him and abruptly walked off.

"He totally is," I said, barely containing my smile.

"Get rid of him immediately," my father snapped at me. "I will not have a rude son-in-law. You need to show some respect, son."

Greg showed his full display of teeth.

I was also satisfied to see that Greg was a hair taller than my father.

"I only show respect to people who are superior to me," Greg said. "And so far in life, I had never found anyone that fits the bill until Belle."

"This is why I told you to come home," my father barked at me. "You're out here gallivanting around and shacking up with sociopaths. This man doesn't like you; he doesn't find you attractive. He's just using you."

"You know what they say, women tend to marry men like their fathers," I said dryly.

"How dare you insult me? I will deal with you later," he hissed, running after my mother.

Greg wrapped an arm around me.

"You really shouldn't have done that," I said, sagging. "My parents could make things difficult for you."

"No, they won't," Greg said simply. "They're irrelevant. Besides, I told you I would take care of you."

"You don't have to." But I still let him wrap his arms around me.

Greg tipped my chin up. "Belle, you are the most beautiful woman I have ever seen. I will have you in my life forever."

He thinks I'm beautiful.

"Are you sure?" I said in a small voice. "You could have any woman you want."

"Belle," Greg gave a rueful laugh, "anyone else isn't going to understand my past. My father is a nutcase, my mother is MIA, and I am responsible for actual litters of younger brothers. Other women are going to think they can just have a normal relationship with me. But you get it. You understand what it's like to be responsible for your brothers. We make sense together. It's only logical."

I chewed on my lip. "So you just want me to help you take care of your brothers?"

"God no," Greg said. "Nothing like that—they don't even live here. They live in Harrogate with my half brother. I meant I'm abstractly responsible for them. Financially. Once they're older and can eat with a knife and a fork, then they come to Manhattan for refinement." He took my arm and continued with me down the street.

"What about your sisters?" I asked after a moment. Darkness settled over Greg's face.

"There's nothing that can be done at the moment. They are where we cannot reach them."

"Nothing?" I spun around to face him. "So you have sisters stuck with your crazy father out in the desert trapped in some doomsday polygamist cult, and you're not helping them."

He looked away. "It's complicated."

"You need to do something about that, or I will," I warned, poking him in the chest with a finger.

"You will?" He raised an eyebrow.

"Yes," I said emphatically. "They're trapped there, and they need to be rescued. And if you're not going to do it, I'll do it."

"You are something else," Greg said, shaking his head.

"It's about doing what's right."

"I have plans in motion," Greg assured me. "My father isn't getting away with his bullshit much longer. But," he added, cutting off my protests, "if you are feeling altruistic, how about a date with me?"

"I'll always go on a date with you," I said then kicked myself. Did I sound too needy?

Greg frowned slightly.

"It's a triple date," he admitted. "I have this potential client; he's a bit of a woo-woo, alternative-spiritual-hipster type, but he wants to have a group date."

"So you want me to go to a business dinner with you," I clarified.

"Only if you want to."

I looked down at my feet. "I don't have anything to wear. I'm not sure if that dress you brought me is appropriate for a business dinner. It may be a bit too fancy."

He leaned down to kiss me. "That's why I'm taking you shopping."

• • • • • • • • • • • • • •

I low-key hate shopping.

My stomach churned with my lunch that I stress ate too fast as I slowly walked with Greg down the street to a nearby boutique.

They aren't going to have anything your size, I reminded myself. *Then it's going to be awkward, and Greg's going to dump you for being a bad corporate girlfriend.*

Seeing my parents had somehow catapulted me back to my teenagerhood. I had this vivid, awful memory of my mother trying to manufacture a rare mother-daughter moment. We had gone to the junior section at the high-end department store, and absolutely nothing fit. My mother berated me that I ate too much and that she was going to have to buy me something from the adult section. However, the clothes there hadn't fit either because my boobs hadn't really come in yet.

I walked up the steps to the boutique, feeling like I was going to my execution.

Greg was going to watch me be humiliated as I was unable to find anything in my size. And the date was tonight, so there was no way I would have time to have anything altered.

Maybe you can just wear a pair of jeans and your black sweater? I thought in a panic.

Except that Dana's cat had chewed a hole in the sweater, and the jeans needed to be washed because I had spilled part of my lasagna on them last week.

"We're looking for a dress for a business dinner," Greg said to the saleslady after she greeted us.

"Any particular style?"

Greg looked at me expectantly.

"Nothing too fancy," I said, trying to sound calm and not like I was about to have a panic attack. "It's about investing, so it should be fairly conservative but still look nice."

And hopefully fit me. Please god, let it fit me. I will totally give up SunChips for a month if something, anything in here fits.

"Let's have a look," the saleswoman said as she showed me around the small store while Greg settled into one of the leather chairs beside the front window to answer emails on his phone. "See anything you like?"

"Lots." But I knew nothing was going to fit me.

You need to pick something! my brain shrieked.

I stopped in front of a model wearing a fuck-me pencil skirt suit with a kick-ass black headband and four-inch stilettoes.

"I low-key love that," I joked.

"Nothing like a power suit! This one is updated from your standard eighties fare," the saleswoman said, pointing to the suit jacket. "It's a one button, but it's been structured so you don't have that random flare out that accentuates a food baby."

I laughed. "Well, I need something for my boyfriend's business dinner. I'm just arm candy; I'm not pitching anything, so it's probably not appropriate."

But when I did eventually pitch a deal, that suit would be so boss.

"How about this dress?" another saleswoman suggested, showing me a strapless green dress with a flouncy sweet skirt and a big bow at the back.

"I'll see if it fits," I said.

I snapped a few pictures of the dress after I had put it on and sent it to my friends.

> **Dana:** *Was that made for you?*
> **Emma:** *That looks fantastic!*
> **Belle:** *It's too short! It came down to the mannequin's knees! On me it stops midthigh, and I think my boobs are going to pop out.*
> **Dana:** *It actually makes it look a little edgy in a good way. You look like a supermodel.*
> **Emma:** *Your legs look a mile long.*
> **Emma:** *Totally loving that ethical THOT style.*
> **Dana:** *You have to wear your heels.*
> **Belle:** *No way! I'll just fall over. I need to wear my lucky flats.*

I chewed on my lip and examined my reflection. I did look sort of pretty.

But what would Greg think?

CHAPTER 24
GREG

I reviewed my notes for the dinner that evening. I would lead with chatting about how great it was to have a girlfriend, maybe some fun anecdotes about how obnoxious dating could be. Belle had some horror stories. Martin would for sure eat it up.

We'd have drinks at the bar. I would pay. I needed to do it in a non-obvious way, though. Best to show up early and give my credit card to the restaurant and have Martin know it was on me after the fact.

Then we could avoid the awkward fight for the bill at the end of the evening.

Belle would need her hair and makeup done. Not too much. I had one of my brothers research the girls Martin and his brother were dating. They seemed like the natural hippy type, so Belle couldn't be too done up. She needed fresh makeup.

After dinner, I would bring up the investment. Martin and Todd weren't going to want to talk business in front of their girlfriends. Maybe I could somehow convince Belle to take the girlfriends to the bar or the restroom or outside, so I could do my pitch. It was a small pitch, just to get Martin and Todd to agree to come to Svensson Investment for a long formal presentation where I would show Martin just how well we would manage his money.

My phone rang. Martin. I got in the zone before I answered it.

"Greg," my man Martin said. "Still on for tonight?"

"Absolutely."

"Good, good. So…" He sighed. "You know little brothers."

"Yes."

"Well, mine is being a complete piece of shit. Ugh, I'm supposed to be using positive language."

"It's fine," I said. "My brothers drive me to drink and swear on a daily basis."

Martin laughed. "Unfortunately, my brother is being a pill. I need to humor him."

"Uh-huh," I said, not sure where this was going.

"Long story short, he doesn't like Belle. She insulted him at one of the dating events. Really, though, I think it's because she's taller than him, and he has a complex and hasn't gotten in touch with his inner strength. He'll be awful to deal with tonight if she's there."

"She can wear flats," I said, making a mental note.

"He's just not going to go for it. He's been complaining about it nonstop."

"She doesn't have to come," I said smoothly, but inside I was cringing. This was not a good look. Belle was going to kill me.

I'll make it up to her.

"Unfortunately, I can't bail on my girlfriend, and my brother already has been talking this triple date up to his current lingerie model he's dating," Martin said. "Could you just bring someone else? Just for tonight. It will just make things easier and make my brother more likely to not fight moving my investment to your firm."

Fuck. He was going to invest with my company. I looked toward the dressing room. The door opened, and I heard Belle's voice.

"I am happy to accommodate," I said smoothly.

"Thanks, dude! Todd's been insufferable. Take Belle somewhere nice, okay? Like take her to Paris for shopping."

"Will do," I said, feeling slightly stunned.

I turned to Belle after I hung up the phone. She looked beautiful—her legs were amazing in the dress, and it framed her shoulders perfectly.

What was I going to say?

"What do you think?" she asked.

Shit.

I twirled her around and pulled her to me.

"I want to fuck you in that dress," I whispered to her.

She giggled.

"Unfortunately," I said, hanging my head, "Martin just called me." I tried to seem as contrite as possible. I was a frighteningly good liar. My father had trained me well. "It seems that his girlfriend broke up with him. It was quite messy, I'm afraid, and he wants to make the business dinner more of a sordid bachelor evening."

"Oh," Belle said, blinking. "Well, that's fine. I'll just go take this off and let you get ready."

I pulled her close to me. "I don't have anything to get ready for. And I'm still buying that dress. I want you riding my dick wearing it."

"Oh!"

While she was changing, I quickly booked a woman from an escort service one of my clients had told me to use. I had never taken him up on it, but he said they promised discretion. And I needed it. There was no way Belle would go for my taking some other woman to this business dinner. I ordered a short brunette. Hopefully, she wouldn't set off Martin's brother.

Fortunately, Belle didn't seem too bent out of shape when she came out of the dressing room.

"I promise," I told her, "I am going to spend the rest of the afternoon making it up to you."

CHAPTER 25
Belle

♡ ♡ ♡

"This is swanky," I said to Greg when the limo pulled up in front of his condo.

"It's serviceable," he said, ushering me inside. "This was the first development Svensson Investment built. Unfortunately, all of the units are occupied by my brothers."

"You must be a close-knit family," I said.

"Too close," he replied as the doorman swiped the key card for the elevator. As soon as the doors shut, Greg grabbed me and kissed me.

I moaned against him as he pushed me against the wall, one leg pushing mine apart.

God, I wanted him.

We stumbled into his condo. I barely had time to register the exposed heavy timber beams, the kitchen that was larger than Emma's apartment, and the floor-to-ceiling, steel-framed windows before he picked me up and took me to his bedroom.

Yes, friends. He literally picked me up.

His gray eyes were dilated, and his normally perfectly parted hair was messy when he pushed me off him and handed me the box from the store. "Put it on."

"It's such a nice dress," I protested.

"Yes," he said, "that's why I want to fuck you in it."

There was dark heat in his eyes, and I felt my own body respond with a flush of heat that seemed to curl into my core. I licked my lips. "Fine. I'll wear the damn dress."

He reached for me, and I half danced out of the way, grinning. He wanted me in a dress? Fine, but he would get a show.

With a low growl, Greg sat on the bed watching me, his hands going to his belt.

That decided it for me: The striptease was on.

Hooking my fingers under the hem of my shirt, I pulled my shirt up and over my head with aching slowness, showing every inch of skin along the way. I threw the clothing to the side, my top clad in only my lacy bra, my hair messy and wild down my back.

"You like what you see?" I asked teasingly.

His gaze lingered for a moment on my bra before sweeping downward. "Show me more."

Oh, I planned to.

I proceeded to unbutton my jeans, pulling the zipper down and slipping my hand in to rub over my pussy. My gaze never left his for a moment.

Greg swallowed. "You wet for me, baby?"

I was definitely on my way. My answer was a smile. "Are you sure you want me in that nice dress? It would be a shame to mess it up."

"I'll buy you another."

The man wanted what the man wanted. Besides, I had ideas of my own.

I lowered my jeans over my hips and panties, kicking away shoes and socks to leave me bare except for my bra.

Then I reached for the dress.

His eyebrows rose, and before he could say anything, I said, "You told me to put on the dress. Not anything else."

"Naughty little girl."

Ha! He called me little!

The dress was silky and felt slippery cool over my flushed skin. Settling it over my mostly naked body, I turned.

"Zip me up?" Greg was up in an instant, his hands floating over my naked back, bunching and unbunching the fabric as if he longed to rip it off me.

I turned my head to look at him over my shoulder and then clucked my tongue. "I thought you wanted me in this dress."

"I do." Finally, he took his hands off me long enough to zip up the back. The slight constriction of the tight fabric was a contrast to the breeze I felt down below.

Greg gripped me by the waist and pulled me into him so tight that I could feel his still-clothed erection press into my ass.

The thought of letting him take me like this, bent over the bed with the skirt of the dress flipped up and him riding me to completion...it was almost enough to make me change my plans.

Fortunately, I had other ideas.

I turned in his arms. Greg leaned in to kiss me, and with a wicked smile, I pushed him back and followed him down onto the bed.

He rose half up to kiss me. Having none of it, I straddled his hips, grinning down at him.

"You like this dress?" I asked innocently.

Greg's hands slid up my thighs to squeeze my bare bottom. "I like what's under it more."

I pretended to pout but couldn't keep up the expression for longer than a moment. "You're overdressed for the occasion..." I reached for his fly.

Greg, smart man that he was, seemed to be completely on board. He lifted his hips, urging me along as I unzipped his fly and drew out his large cock.

My tongue peeped out to wet my lips. The thought of having his hard shaft in my mouth was delightful, but I had already dressed for the occasion.

Finally, I'd take my ride.

"Tell me you have a condom," I said, my voice husky.

Greg reached under himself to his back pocket. I snatched the foil from his hands, opened it, and rolled it over his cock in record speed. I was done playing nice. I wanted him, now.

Condom firmly in place, I grabbed the hem of my dress in one hand, using the other to balance. I settled myself down firmly over him and let the dress spread out as I sank down, taking him in one smooth glide.

He closed his eyes in bliss, and I had to work not to do the same. Fuck, he was so large, so hot up inside me... so perfect. I rose up again, taking him down to the hilt inside me just to feel the stretch—just to feel how close we were joined.

His hands landed on my hips, helping to guide me, moving as I rocked up and down on top of him. Our pace was unhurried—each of us enjoying the ride. It was sinful, in a way—as if my dress were covering up a pleasurable little secret.

But I could not hold back the tide of ecstasy for long. Greg canted his hips up, hitting me perfectly on my downstroke. I moaned, clenching, rising and falling, to feel it again... and again...

"Please..." I cried out, not sure why. I was the one directing this show. But then his hands tightened against me hard, holding me in place as he fucked up into me. I moaned, my legs spread wide to take everything he would give me—gravity pushing us more joined than we ever were before.

I came, moaning. His dick seemed to stiffen just a touch more. Then he, too, was coming. He pulled the dress off me the rest of the way then cradled me naked against his chest, pressing soft kisses to my skin.

"Don't ever leave me," Greg whispered to me.

• • • • • • • • • • • • • • •

I woke a few hours later. Greg was moving around the bedroom, skin slightly damp, a towel around his waist.

"Unfortunately, I have to go deal with my client," he said, "though I would much rather stay here with you."

"I think my dress is wrinkled," I murmured, looking at it down on the floor.

"No matter. I plan on ripping it off you when I get back," he said.

He leaned over me, pressing a kiss to my mouth then peppering kisses along my collarbone to my tits. I ran my hand down his bare chest then lower, satisfied with the sounds he made when I stroked the length of his cock.

"I'm seriously considering throwing this deal just to fuck you," he murmured.

"I should probably get some work done anyway," I said. "I need to decide if I'm going to invest in the cupcake company or the dog biscuit company." I gave him a coy smile. "Do you know the answer?"

"Cupcakes," he said with a smile.

"Wrong. Dog biscuits," I said as he dropped the towel. I admired his muscular torso as he pulled on his black boxer briefs then undershirt.

"People will always spend their disposable income on their dogs and their kids. There are a few developments around town I have been looking at. Several have pet boutiques, and it's obscene the amount of money they bring in. They have the smallest footprints, and they're some of the highest-grossing stores."

"Fascinating insight," Greg said, frowning as he finished dressing while I greatly enjoyed the show.

He stood in front of the mirror and fastened his cuff links then his tie. He turned back to face me as he put on his jacket.

"I have food in the fridge for you," he told me. "I don't think this will take long, so don't go anywhere."

"I'm not planning to," I said, swinging my feet off the bed and wrapping the sheet around me. I'd always seen that done in the movies and wanted to do it.

Greg stroked me through the thin cotton fabric, and I padded after him to the kitchen.

"This place is a bit small, but make yourself at home."

"The fact that I can stretch out and not touch two opposite walls at the same time makes this condo a palace in my book!" I told him, giving him one last kiss before he left.

My phone beeped with a series of text messages right as I was about to hop into the shower.

> **Dana:** *Can you run by our new office space? The landlord says he left some paperwork there for us to sign, and he's a million years old and refuses to email it over.*
>
> **Dana:** *The entrance is the stairwell right next to that swanky new Japanese place.*
>
> **Belle:** *Can I do it tomorrow? I'll be heading back that way from Greg's place.*
>
> **Emma:** *Greg's place?!?!?!*
>
> **Dana:** *As proud as I am of you for exploring your inner sex goddess, he wants them back by the morning, and I need to review then sign.*
>
> **Belle:** *Okay, I'll head over.*
>
> **Emma:** *Is no one going to talk about how Greg freaking Svensson had Belle over at his place, and you're just going to leave him!*
>
> **Emma:** *Shit. I'll go get the papers myself.*
>
> **Dana:** *You said you have a macaroni and cheese and chocolate cake fest planned tonight, and you were not taking off your unicorn onesie for anything.*
>
> **Emma:** *I mean I will do it so that Belle isn't peacing out on her new billionaire boy toy.*

Belle: *He actually had a business thing to go to so I'll grab the papers, scan them, and send to you.*
Emma: *A business thing?!*
Belle: *Yes, because he is a businessman, not a mooch. It comes with the territory.*
Emma: *His dick better be very nice if you're totally cool with him just ditching you.*
Belle: **Smiley face emoji* It is very nice!*

• • • • • • • • • • • •

Our new office space wasn't all that far away from Greg's condo. I decided to walk, enjoying the cold air against my skin.

The papers were in the mailbox inside the door where Dana had said. I flipped through them as I walked past the Japanese restaurant. It did look like a nice place. I peered in. Maybe I should suggest to Greg that we go there tomorrow.

I narrowed my eyes and leaned in, my nose almost pressing to the glass, not daring to believe what I was seeing.

Was that Greg? Surely not. Surely it was one of his brothers.

Because there at the table was a tall, blond man with a woman—a short, petite, cute woman who lovingly reached her hand up to stroke along his jaw, who he softly smiled down at, who was feminine and sweet and was wearing four-inch heels but didn't even come up to his chin.

"What the fuck!" I yelled against the glass.

The man turned, and Greg's eyes flashed up and met mine.

Fuck, he mouthed.

CHAPTER 26

GREG

The escort met me outside the restaurant at the appointed time. She was very short. I had to crane my neck down to talk to her.

"I take payment up front," she said. "Your bank account has already been debited, FYI."

"Of course."

"We are a girlfriend service, not a prostitution service," she said flatly, "and there will be no funny business."

"Certainly not," I told her.

"Good," she said and looked at me expectantly.

I offered her my arm.

"Thanks, *babe*! I'm really looking forward to meeting your clients!"

• • • • • • • • • • • •

The escort was worth the high price tag.

Martin and his brother walked into the restaurant ten minutes later.

"Thanks, man," Martin whispered as he shook my hand.

His brother scowled at the escort while his girlfriend started peppering her with inane questions about astrology. The escort held her own and distracted the other two women and Martin's brother while I chatted with Martin.

"I've been doing a little asking around town," he said as we accepted our drinks from the bartender.

"Everyone seems impressed with your investment firm's portfolio. I also really appreciate the fact that you and several of your brothers who are involved either have started successful companies or currently run them. I don't like these investment firms where it's just some rando gambling with his trust fund."

Martin laughed. "If I wanted that, I could do it myself!"

"It looks like the table is ready, boys," my fake girlfriend said.

I offered her my arm, and we made our way through the restaurant.

"When did you two meet?" Martin's brother asked with a scowl.

"We've been friends a long time, haven't we, Greg?" the escort lied smoothly. "I just flew back in town from Paris and randomly ran into him at a bar, and we decided to give it a go." She reached up to stroke my face. "He's always so busy with his investing that I'm shocked he has time for me at all. I might have to crash some more client meetings to get time with him!"

I laughed along with everyone else.

"Come sit by me," the escort cooed to Martin's brother, allowing me to sit across from Martin.

As I helped her into her seat, I looked across the restaurant to the windows fronting the street. There, like a vengeful winter spirit, was Belle.

Fuck.

"Excuse me. I'll be right back," I said, making up a lie on the spot. "It seems like one of my younger brothers almost, uh, burned down the house."

Fuck, fuck, fuck!

What was she doing here?

Belle was furious when I rushed out of the restaurant. I grabbed her arm to try and haul her away from the window.

But she dug her feet in.

"Belle, please," I begged, trying to maneuver her. "Just let me explain."

"I don't really want to hear any of it," she said, wrenching her arm away.

"She's not someone I'm dating," I said in a rush, "I'm trying to land this contract, and Martin's brother doesn't like you because you're too tall, so I needed someone else."

Tears pricked in her eyes.

"Right," she said, chin starting to wobble. "So you found a short, cute girl so that I wouldn't embarrass you."

"No, not like that. I love you," I assured her. "You're stunning and beautiful—"

"Just not enough to take on one of your business dinners." She turned her head away. "God, you're just like my father, you know that? Manipulative and a liar."

"No, I'm not," I retorted. "I'm trying to run a business; it was a business decision. Martin Shaw is the biggest contract this year. Everyone is after him. And I have a shot. He's making a decision in the next couple of days. My company is a shoo-in unless I blow this evening. I had to do what I had to do. That's how it is. You're not in investing, so you wouldn't understand."

"Yes, I am," she snapped.

"Not like I am." I blew out a breath, and it fogged in front of me like a smoke screen. "There's twenty billion dollars on the line here. I have to win this contract."

She held out her arms.

"Fine," she said. "If money is that important to you, then have at it."

"Stop being so high and mighty," I snarled at her. "Money is important. You wouldn't know because you didn't grow up poor like I did. We didn't have running water. The power was wind generated and would randomly stop working. My parents hated me and my siblings, and I was responsible for my younger brothers. I still am. I'm doing this for them. I have to take care of my little brothers; I can't abandon them."

"You mean like I did?" she shrieked at me, the tears starting to stream down her face.

"I'm not saying that. I'm just saying this is bigger than a date. I will take you to Paris. I will take you to Milan. I will buy you a penthouse. I'm sorry, Belle. I know this looks like shit, but I will make it up to you later. I swear it."

She glared at me, eyes like a frozen lake.

"Don't bother," she said. "Enjoy your dinner."

She turned and walked off quickly.

Run after her.

Except that I had to score this contract. I had been gone too long already.

"I'll make it up to you!" I yelled after Belle.

Fuck.

CHAPTER 27
Belle

♡ ♡ ♡

"I thought you were going to scan these forms in?" Dana said when Emma ushered me into her apartment.

"Turns out I had a little more free time on my hands, after all," I said bitterly then burst into tears. "Greg said I was too tall."

"That dick!" Emma cried, hugging me.

"How are you too tall for him? The Svensson brothers are all ginormous," Dana said from her perch on the cardboard-box coffee table.

"He went out for a client dinner and brought some pretty, petite, short girl as his date. He lied to me about it. He said his client broke up with his girlfriend, and they were having a guys' night, but he just didn't want to be seen out in public with me. God, I feel so stupid. I should have known," I sobbed into the shoulder of Emma's pink unicorn onesie.

"Jeez," I wiped my face with the back of my sleeve. "I swore I wasn't going to let a man have this much power over me ever again, yet here I am. What the hell is wrong with me? Maybe Greg was right—I don't have it in me to be an investment powerhouse."

"Oh hell no!" Emma said, wagging one of the sparkling hooves of her onesie at me. "You cut that negativity out right now, Dana! The macaroni and cheese."

Dana looked at her askance.

"The pasta, Dana!" Emma demanded.

Dana rolled her eyes and brought over the casserole dish.

Emma scooped out a big spoonful and stuffed it into my mouth.

"You," she said as I chewed, "are going to grow a pair of ovaries. We," she said, motioning between the three of us, "have it in us to be some of the most powerful investors in the city. We just need to believe in ourselves."

"That's not how it works," Dana said in annoyance.

"I'm glad you actually showed up," Dana said to me. "Emma called me over here trying to convince me to go along with this scheme of hers to go after the Martin Shaw account that literally everyone in the nation wants. They've been wining and dining this joker for weeks."

"We have to try. Tell her!" Emma pleaded.

"Dana's right," I said, slumping on Emma's bed. "Greg is going after that contract. That's who he was meeting with tonight. It sounds like he thinks he has it in the bag."

"It's not over until there's a signature on a contract," Emma said, slamming her onesie hooves on the linoleum countertop.

"We're just going to look stupid," I said.

"No, we aren't," Emma said emphatically. "Because we are going to have a stupidly awesome pitch! We are scoring that account. And we are going to stick it to Greg and make him weep when he realizes he lost both Belle and his precious contract. Ladies, get out your spreadsheets!"

• • • • • • • • • • • • •

I had to admit, after gallons of coffee and working on our presentation, that it did seem legit. Emma had been working on the numbers and market projections for the past several weeks, and I had also been doing research on various underserved market sectors.

Dana produced some great graphics, and we made a pretty convincing case for investing in niche markets that ranged from being hyper-targeted to women to being inspired by things various women-centric markets would go for.

"How are we even going to get a meeting with Martin Shaw?" I said. "Does anyone even know where he has his office?"

"I've been stalking him," Emma said happily.

"Oh lord," Dana said.

"Why?" I asked, incredulous.

"Because I told you from day one we needed to go after his account. I'm BFFs with the receptionist in the work-share space he's in. I already texted her, and she said he's usually there in the mornings. She said ten was probably a good time."

"We have a couple of hours," Dana said. "I'm going home to shower and change." She closed her laptop.

"Everyone needs to look sharp," she warned. "Look like you could manage a twenty-billion-dollar account."

"I don't have anything to wear," I complained after she left. I had never held a real corporate job. The only nice things I owned were the dresses Greg had bought me.

He's dead to me.

"You need a power suit!" Emma said, taking out her own suit from her Wall Street days. "We should go shopping. It can be a business expense."

"I don't know, Emma."

"And you have to wear heels."

"Oh no!" I said emphatically. "Greg already told me that he didn't bring me along because of my height. I'm definitely wearing flats."

Emma rolled her eyes. "Fine, but you still need a suit."

She searched on her phone while I showered. "I found three recommended stores that cater to tall women."

"Actually," I said, wringing out my hair, "I already know a place that has a nice suit."

• • • • • • • • • • • • • •

The saleswomen greeted me when I walked into the boutique. "How was your business dinner last night?"

"Terrible," I told them. "And now I need that suit I was looking at yesterday."

Except yesterday, Greg had been paying. I looked at the price tag and winced.

"Business expense!" Emma said. "YOLO!"

"That's like my entire credit card limit."

"Just try it on," she coaxed.

I pulled on the suit in the dressing room.

"It's not going to fit. You're going to look stupid," I told myself. But when I turned to look in the mirror, I looked…

Not just hot—I looked dangerous and sexy. "Dayum, that's a nice suit."

I put my hair up in a bun and slid on the headband.

Emma applauded when I walked out of the dressing room. Dana, who had arrived while I was changing, raised an eyebrow.

"It's missing something," she said, tapping her chin.

"Shoes," the saleswoman said.

Emma grinned maniacally and pulled the heels out of her bag. "You have to!"

"I can't walk in those!" I protested as Emma ran to put them on the floor in front of me.

"Heel toe, heel toe," Dana instructed as I slipped into them.

They felt like they were made for me.

"Yes!" Emma cheered as I walked around the store. "Greg is going down!"

• • • • • • • • • • • • •

It was hard not to feel like a total boss in the outfit. Dana had even lent me one of her designer Birkin bags—black.

I forced myself to project calm while Emma chatted with the receptionist and slid her a container of caramel marshmallow brownies she had made.

"These are life changing," Emma promised.

The receptionist beamed. "Martin's not in a meeting. Let me walk you back."

We trailed her through the shared workspace. My heels clacked on the polished hardwood floor, the sound echoing off the reclaimed brick walls.

"Martin?" the receptionist said sweetly, poking her head into the little glass box where Martin Shaw had his work area. "I have a few ladies here who want to talk to you about investment."

"Oh!" Martin's eyes bugged out of his head when he saw us. A man I recognized as his brother Todd from the dating event scowled.

Ugh. This was not going to go well. I was regretting it already. And I had already taken the tags off the suit. I was going to be out all that money. What had I been thinking?

But Emma was prepared.

"Wheatgrass smoothie?" she chirped. "I made it myself."

"Homemade?" Martin said, perking up.

His brother's scowl grew deeper. "I don't know why you keep drinking that crap."

Emma pulled a second plate of brownies out of her bag. "And for those who are not on the healthy food train."

Mollified somewhat, Martin's brother didn't protest when I said, "We heard that you were looking for someone to manage your fund. We wanted to give you the opportunity to consider our investment firm."

"We have had a ton of people come through here already," Todd complained.

"Yes, but I am making the decision," Martin told him.

"You can't just unilaterally make the decision!"

"I can," Martin declared.

Dana and I looked at each other as the two brothers squabbled.

"Boys," I said sharply. It was the same tone I would use to get my brothers in line.

They snapped to attention.

"Martin, why can't Todd have a say in the decision?" I asked.

"Because my granddad left me in charge," he said. "Todd doesn't get to manage the trust until he's thirty. Which is another five years from now."

"Martin's trying to hand off our money to all these rando investment firms. You should see the skeezy people he's brought through here," Todd told me. "And he didn't ask my opinion at all!"

"Both of you sit down and eat your snack," I said. "Show me the other investment proposals people have given you. We'll sort it out together."

Like little puppies, they handed over glossy brochures and binders full of photographs of creepily smiling Wall Street sociopaths.

Dana, Emma, and I went through them one by one.

"Don't use them," Emma said. "They aren't even solvent."

"These guys have shorted half the companies in the US," Dana said, tossing another binder in the trash. "Terrible."

"Unimaginative."

We went through the whole pile as Martin and his brother looked on. Then we came to the Svensson Investment packet.

I flipped through it.

"Could be fine," I said.

Martin's brother was suspicious. "Aren't you Greg Svensson's girlfriend?"

"Ex," I clarified. "And we were barely even dating."

I tapped a number on one of the foldout spreadsheets.

"They are probably capable of giving you this good of a return," I said. "But I think you two would rather have a more hands-on approach and work with people who are only managing your accounts, not half of New England's."

Martin was nodding along.

"We can give you a custom-tailored development package," Dana said smoothly, pulling up our presentation.

"We have a number of market sectors we've identified as being underserved," Dana continued. "There are still undeveloped parcels of land along the Hudson. We advise building developments that have a unique identity. Simultaneously, we will also invest in businesses that will serve underserved women-dominated markets. There is huge demand in women-centered alcohol sales, software, and app services. And of course media, which our media company, Romance Creative, has already tapped into."

"Sounds fine, but I want to help!" Todd said.

"You can't," Martin told him. "That's the point of why we're hiring an investment firm."

"Stop being mean to your brother. He can help," I told Martin.

"He'll lose all the money."

"We won't let it get that far. But you can come to some of the meetings," I promised Todd.

"Yes!" He pumped a fist.

Martin rolled his eyes. "I'll think about it and get back to you."

"No, you need to decide together," I said. "You're brothers. All you will have ultimately is each other. Don't ruin your relationship over money."

"Okay, okay," he said begrudgingly.

"Hug it out," I ordered.

Martin embraced his brother. "I love you, man."

"I love you too."

"Adorable," Dana said.

CHAPTER 28
GREG

"Today's the big day," Hunter said when I walked into the office the next morning.

The meeting yesterday had gone perfectly. I had pitched to Martin, and he had requested a packet, which I couriered over to be waiting for him at his office this morning. I was supposed to come in at eleven thirty and discuss.

I straightened my tie in the mirror.

I was going to win this contract, then I was going to grovel to Belle. Should I take her on a big trip? Maybe I should just skip right to it and buy her a place to live. That should smooth things over. No one in their right mind said no to a free piece of property in New York City.

"Carl," I said to my younger brother, "find me a decent one-bedroom condo for purchase. Actually, make it two bedrooms. Make sure it has a balcony and is in a safe building."

He saluted and handed me and Hunter copies of the pitch book I'd had him courier over to Martin.

"I already have the champagne ordered for when you get back," he said.

• • • • • • • • • • • • • •

"You sure are confident," Hunter remarked as the car parked in front of the Shaws' office.

"I had a great meeting yesterday. Martin all but told me that we were getting the contract."

"I looked over Archer and Mike's hotel proposals," Hunter said, "and I wouldn't proceed with the 58th Street property, but I would with the other two."

"Mike seems to think he can make all three of them work," I told him as we rode the elevator up.

"We'll see about that," Hunter said. "I don't trust your judgment. Beck said that you've been acting out of sorts lately, what with your new girlfriend and all, disappearing at all hours of the night."

I pulled open the glass door to the shared workspace.

"Speaking of," Hunter murmured.

I seethed. I could just feel Hunter smirking next to me as I was confronted with Belle.

She didn't look how she normally did. She wasn't wearing one of the flouncy dresses I had bought her or the more casual jeans and sweater she usually wore.

No, she was in a suit—sleek with a crisp white shirt, a black suit jacket in the same fabric as the pencil skirt that was practically glued to her thighs, and a wide belt at the waist that gave her a perfect hourglass figure. Her legs were a mile long in the black patent-leather stilettos.

"Good morning, Greg," Belle said.

I couldn't quite read her expression. I also couldn't quite form words. Belle looked fucking amazing. She was everything I had ever wanted.

I'm going to tell Carl to get a three-bedroom. Maybe four.

"Belle Frost, I presume," Hunter said.

She walked over, heels clicking on the floor. When she brushed past me, she was practically my height.

I want to fuck her in those heels and nothing else.

She shook Hunter's hand. My half brother eyed her warily, then he looked to her friends—a shorter, plump girl and, *shit*, Dana Holbrook. I could already feel Hunter doing the calculations.

"Looking at office space here?" I asked, hoping beyond hope that's why she was there.

"Hardly," she said. "I don't really do sharing."

Shit. She was still mad at me.

"Look," I said, lowering my voice. "Can we please just talk? I have an important meeting right now, but if you could just wait maybe an hour—"

"Greg!" Martin said happily, coming out from the depths of the shared workspace into the lobby area.

"We're a little early," I told him.

"I was actually going to call you, but maybe it's better to tell you in person," he said, rubbing his arm. "I very much appreciate getting to know you and your firm over the past few weeks. I feel like you and I have really bonded over the whole dating experience, and I would like for us to remain friends. However, we're going with the Artemis Investment firm to manage our fund."

Glass shattering. I reeled.

Keep it together.

"I… see…"

I could tell Hunter was livid beside me.

Trying not to seem shaken, I pulled myself together.

"We appreciate your consideration, Martin. We actually didn't know there was a new fund in town." I glanced over at Belle, who wore a triumphant look on her face.

"They're new, and they made an excellent pitch," Martin said, beaming.

"Besides," he added, "my spiritual advisor said that what I was really lacking in my life was a strong woman, one who was no-nonsense and who would take charge—a real straight shooter. Belle and her firm were the only ones to come in and knock us down a peg."

"Yep," his brother said, snickering. "It was actually really awesome to see her yell at Martin."

"I thought you said she was too tall," I hissed at Todd.

"Yeah, to date," he said, "but I mean, look at her. Wouldn't you want her dominating your money?"

"*What the fuck*," I muttered.

Hunter elbowed me in the ribs.

"We appreciate your consideration and wish you all the best with your endeavors," Martin said. "Please let us know if there's any way we can assist you further."

"Still friends?" Martin said, holding out his arms.

"Of course," I replied, voice sounding hollow.

Martin gave me a big hug.

His brother handed me a napkin-wrapped brownie.

"Artemis Investment brought these," he said. "They are life changing."

"And I'm sending you the info to my spiritual advisor," Martin told me, pressing his hands together. "She's taking new clients."

"Well," I said, forcing a professional smile on my face, "good luck, ladies."

"We don't need luck," Belle said. "It's just math and careful study of the market."

●●●●●●●●●●●●●

The entire car ride back to the office, Hunter didn't say a word. I sat beside him in shock.

Belle won that contract? The contract everyone in Manhattan was going after. Why? How?

Hunter's anger was almost tangible in the elevator cab as we rode up to my office.

"Look," I said to him as we approached the eighty-third floor. "I don't know what happened."

The elevator doors opened.

"You did it!" several of my brothers yelled as champagne corks popped.

Liam threw a handful of glitter at me then saw the anger etched on Hunter's face. "Oh shit."

"'Good luck, ladies'?" Hunter turned and roared at me, the dam holding back his anger disintegrating. "No fucking wonder Belle turned around and screwed you over if that's how you behave around women."

"What?" Carl said, taking off his party hat. "Belle got the contract? How?"

"I would assume," Hunter sneered, "that she, like Greg, was at those ridiculous dating events to get close to Martin. Then she probably saw that Greg was slow and stupid and an easy mark and used his infatuation with her to steal our ideas and counteract them with a perfectly tailored pitch."

"I don't know about that," I said.

"Did you never even ask her what she did for a living?" Hunter fumed at me.

"I... she said she had an investment firm, but it was just something stupid," I rambled. "I mean, they were meeting at a restaurant, for god's sake. She was going to invest in a cupcake shop and a dog grooming business."

"She was with a Holbrook," Hunter snarled.

"I didn't know they were friends," I protested.

"They were probably working with her to screw us over," Hunter continued, face screwed up in fury. "And you just sat there and let it happen!"

Crawford started laughing. "You fucking dick. She played your ass."

"They are trying to ruin our company! Why the hell are you laughing?" Hunter yelled at Crawford.

"It wasn't about our company," I said, sagging. "She just did it to get back at me. I sort of fucked up."

I looked up at the ceiling and blew out a breath. "Martin's brother said he didn't want Belle at the dinner on Thursday, so I lied and told her that girlfriends weren't allowed. And then I brought a pretend girlfriend."

Crawford slapped his thigh. "You asshole! You brought an escort."

"She was more of an actress."

"Escort," Crawford shot back.

"Look, Belle was just jealous. She probably just waltzed in there, made some big promises to Martin, and he's so out of it that he just ate it up. I'm sure she and her friends are way over their heads. I'm going to go over there and apologize because, unlike Hunter, I am absolutely capable of doing that. Then I'll offer to have Svensson Investment partner with Artemis Investment and manage the fund.

Maybe we won't get all the capital, but it will be a large enough percentage. It will be fine. They're probably out celebrating right now, so I'll wait until later and swing by Belle's office when she's a little tipsy and more amenable to suggestions."

Crawford narrowed his eyes. "You are a fucking piece of shit, you know that?"

"Yes, but I always win in the end."

CHAPTER 29
Belle

♡ ♡ ♡

"Did we just win that big-ass contract because the Shaw brothers have some sort of financial dominatrix fantasy going on about Belle?" Emma joked later that evening after we had spent some time with Martin and Todd going over the accounts, signing contracts, then strategizing amongst ourselves on our next moves.

We had a lot more work to do, but now we were celebrating!

"Money is money," Dana said, pouring out another round of champagne.

"Greg probably wants you to be his financial dominatrix," Emma teased, dropping a raspberry in each glass of champagne. "His eyes practically rolled out of his head when he saw you."

"You do look hot in that suit," Dana said, handing me a glass of champagne.

"You definitely put him in his place!" Emma toasted me. "Just make sure he doesn't get too meek in the makeup sex."

"What? I'm not taking him back," I scoffed. "He can go find some other girl."

"You can't just throw him out now after you got him all trained up," Dana said, clicking her tongue. "You're going to have to start all the way from zero if you find another guy."

"Besides, both of you are in finance. Big finance," Emma said excitedly. "Greg's actually perfect for you because he's not going to be intimidated by your success."

"He brought another girl to dinner," I said, shocked that my friends were so ready to forgive and forget.

"And you stole his twenty-billion-dollar contract out from under him," Dana countered. "Now he knows what's what, and he can properly worship you for the goddess you are."

"I don't know…"

"It's because you just had sex last night," Emma said sagely. "Three days from now, you're going to want him back, so you might as well get it over with."

Someone rang the doorbell to the door of our office.

"Speak of the handsome devil," Dana said with a smirk.

I set down my glass, wiped my hands, then went out into the hallway to talk to Greg.

He tracked my motions as I walked over to him, heels clacking on the marble floors.

I could get used to the sound.

"Belle," he said, voice syrupy. "I came to see if you wanted to talk."

"Sure," I said, feeling slightly suspicious. He didn't seem angry or anything.

"Looks like you won a big investment deal, after all."

"Martin and Todd liked my pitch."

"I think they liked the brownies you sent over," Greg said.

Fucking asshole.

"But," he continued, "I know I deserved having the contract yanked away from me. I'm impressed that you managed to secure the fund."

He rested his fingers lightly on my sleeve. "I know this is quite a lot of money, and you're probably overwhelmed with how to handle it. I wanted to let you know that Svensson Investment is happy to help you find the best ways to get good returns."

"Actually," I said, yanking my arm back, "I think we're good."

"Belle," Greg said with a slight laugh, "you can't possibly have the experience to manage this amount of money. It's twenty billion dollars."

"We already have projects in the works," I said stubbornly. "We have a great team, and we're planning on bringing on a few more members who specialize in real estate, retail, and other sectors we're interested in pursuing. But thanks for your concern."

"I'm trying to save you from yourself," he hissed.

"And here I thought you came to grovel," I retorted.

"Grovel?" he spat. "You're the one who needs to apologize."

"Excuse me?"

"Admit it," Greg said harshly. "Especially since you seem to already have your investment pursuits planned out. You were only dating me to steal my intel and go after Martin yourself."

"Actually," I said, glaring at him, "I wasn't. I, for some reason, liked you. Shockingly, I am apparently a walking cliché and went after a man exactly like my father."

"Not this again," Greg huffed. "I'm not the sociopath. You are. You used me."

"I didn't use you!" I screamed at him. "I actually liked you! I liked being around you. I believed you when you said that you wanted me. I believed you when you said I was beautiful. I believed you when you said you wanted me in your life forever."

"And I believed you when you said you were just dabbling in investing, investing in cupcake shops and the like." He glared at me.

"I never said that," I shrieked, stabbing a finger at him. "I always told you I was serious about investing. You constantly belittled me and my ideas. You treated me like I was a naive little girl who needed a big strong investor to tell her how to run her business. You assumed I was useless. I just proved you wrong."

"You haven't proved anything," Greg snarled, face inches from mine, our eyes almost level. "So you won the fund. Good luck increasing it even ten percent, let alone doubling it or tripling it or whatever ludicrous number you told Martin you could achieve."

"And you still don't think I can do it," I said quietly.

"I didn't say that," he said tersely then ran a hand through his hair.

"Look," he said, "clearly we both did things we regret and made mistakes."

"Speak for yourself," I said, crossing my arms. "I'm not sorry for winning the contract. I don't regret it one bit."

"Belle," Greg said, eyes suddenly sad and regretful, "I was just angry. I lost. I hate losing." A wry smile. "I'm probably more like my father than I care to admit. I didn't mean any of that. Please, I don't want to lose you. You're the best thing to ever happen to me. You're beautiful and smart and intelligent. Obviously it is impressive that Martin trusted you with his money. I'm sorry I was being such a dick."

Part of me wanted to forgive him.

Just do it.

But then he opened his big mouth again. "And of course you wanted to prove to me that you could do it. Message received."

Asshole.

"News flash, Greg. My winning the contract wasn't about you. I wasn't even thinking about you at all," I lied. "Like you said, it wasn't personal. It was just business. And since you clearly can't keep the two separate, you need to get out of my office."

•••••••••••••

I felt exhausted when I walked back into the office.

"Are you about to go have crazy makeup sex?" Emma asked hopefully.

I drained my champagne glass.

"No," I said. "I'm going to figure out how to turn our investment firm into the biggest goddamn thing in this city. Fuck Greg."

CHAPTER 30

GREG

"Let me guess," Crawford drawled. "It didn't work."

"Fuck you," I said, feeling exhausted. I numbly undid my jacket, took it off, then lay down on the couch in my office.

"How about a pity scotch," Crawford said, going to the wet bar in my office. But at that moment, several dozen of my younger brothers stampeded around the corner, some of them jumping on the couch and tumbling over me.

"Oops!"

"Sorry, Greg."

"Hi, Greg!"

"It's Greg!" Liam shouted, chasing after them. "Be careful where you jump on him, or you won't have any nephews or nieces."

"I think Greg probably nuked all of that from orbit," Crawford said, handing me a glass of amber-colored scotch.

"So he's back to his old grouch self again?" Liam said. "Too bad."

"And it's too bad you never do any work. You just stir up chaos," I snapped at him.

"Yep, Greg's back!" Liam said cheerfully.

"At the rate you're going, you need to be nice to your brothers," Crawford told me. "We're the only people who are willing to tolerate you and your bullshit."

"She wouldn't even accept my apology," I complained.

"Was it sincere?" Crawford raised a scarred eyebrow.

"Of course," I replied. "I mean, I said I was sorry. She's just refusing to see reason. I'm just going to give her a few weeks to cool off then I'll try again."

"You're going to try again?" Hunter said from the doorway, voice raised over the playful screaming of our younger half brothers.

"I've heard your non apologies, Greg," Hunter spat. "You're lucky she didn't call the police on you. You need to get it in your head that you're not winning Belle back. You nuked that bridge from orbit. I saw her at Martin's office— she was out for blood. You need to stop antagonizing her before she takes down half our company."

"I didn't ask you for your opinion," I growled at him.

"You're getting defensive because you know I'm right."

I refused to believe it. I drained the rest of the glass then got off the couch to stand in front of the window. I was Greg Svensson. I didn't lose. I loved Belle. She would realize it. She would come back to me. I would have her back. Wouldn't I?

I had to.

The alternative would be unbearable.

CHAPTER 31
Belle

♡ ♡ ♡

It had been three weeks since I'd broken up with Greg.

Emma had insisted that the best way to get over him was to go on a date.

Except that was making it worse.

"And you know," the guy across the table from me was saying, "I saw how easy it was to get into the skin-care industry, and I was like, Yeah, I can just throw some money at this, pay off a few Instagram thots, and bada bing bada boom, I'm making millions."

Instagram thots?

Bada bing bada boom?

Greg would despise this guy.

I despised this guy.

He took a bite of his sandwich and continued to talk as he chewed his food.

I desperately wished Greg would show up like he had before and rescue me.

You are not relying on a man ever again, I scolded myself. *You don't need a man. You just won a big contract. Woman up and rescue yourself.*

"Actually," I told the guy, interrupting his tirade about how retail investors were screwing up his friend's hedge fund, "an emergency just came up at work. I have to run. I'll pay for my half at the counter."

I hadn't brought a jacket, but it was late January now, and it had grown colder. Maybe I would buy a nice jacket, a trench coat, maybe, all black.

The winter wind blew through the narrow city streets. Snow flurries were in the air. It was dark and lonely, though there was a smattering of people out. I had just leased an apartment and didn't even have Emma's small but cozy flat to return to.

Shit, I didn't have so much as a houseplant.

I hadn't even had time to shop for furniture. I had been working so much, both because I didn't want to mess up our contract and, of course, to forget Greg—to try to stop myself from missing him, to keep myself from reaching for my phone whenever it chimed, to stop wishing he would text me.

"Is this going to be the rest of my life?" I whispered.

Only the wind answered.

"Stop being such a sad sack. It's lonely at the top," I reminded myself.

This is worth it. Isn't it?

To be continued...

Acknowledgements

A big thank you to Red Adept Editing for editing and proofreading.

And finally a big thank you to all the readers! I had a great time writing this hilarious book! Please try not to choke on your wine while reading!!!

About the Author

If you like steamy romantic comedy novels with a creative streak, then I'm your girl!

Architect by day, writer by night, I love matcha green tea, chocolate, and books! So many books…

Sign up for my mailing list to get special bonus content, free books, giveaways, and more!

http://alinajacobs.com/mailinglist.html

Made in United States
North Haven, CT
06 October 2022